CHILDREN OF OUR OWN WAR

A Boy's Journey

Fred Bonisch

authorHOUSE®

AuthorHouse™
1663 Liberty Drive
Bloomington, IN 47403
www.authorhouse.com
Phone: 1-800-839-8640

First published by AuthorHouse   2/11/2011

ISBN: 978-1-4259-4635-7 (sc)
ISBN: 978-1-4259-4634-0 (hc)

Library of Congress Control Number: 2006905625

Printed in the United States of America

Author of: "The Universe, is it guiding our lives?"

Contents

Foreword

The events described in this book are of my earliest childhood years and took place during World War II and the subsequent postwar years in Germany. Although these events took place some sixty years ago, beginning at an early age of five, they have remained in my memory to this very day. Some of the events may not follow the exact sequence described. They occurred nonetheless. They are part of my childhood memories, and in spite of the troubled times, remain some of my most cherished treasures.

Even now, when I visit the hometown of my youth, I occasionally find myself stopping at a particular corner to allow a childhood event to play out in my mind. At that moment, I feel transformed as my memory provides a replay of an event from so many years ago.

It is important for the reader to understand that the events described are not intended to place blame. Nor should they be compared with others' suffering, which was far greater than ours. Instead, they were real situations we experienced as victims of our own war, and are presented as seen through the eyes of a young boy. History books remind us of the battles, the victories or defeats; however, too little is written about the most innocent and defenseless who often find themselves in the middle of such wars. Seldom do we look at the families back home whose fight it is to survive both starvation and destruction. While the able men are taken away, women alone face the responsibility to care for their families and their survival. There are no medals of heroism or parades to honor them, yet their fights and courage are no less important.

My family, together with many others, has lived through such a period, and so it inspired me to write about those early days. While doing so, I have experienced them once again, even if only in my memory. As children we could often escape into our own world of play and fantasy, even if only for brief periods before facing the next moment of fear. Our mothers did not have this freedom, as worry and fear were always present. It is to their **quiet and unsung heroism and their unwavering dedication to their families that I wish to bring recognition and so dedicate this book.**

I came to the United States in 1959 at the age of twenty and have made it my home. The decision to do so was greatly inspired by having lived under the American occupation of troops at the end of and immediately following World War II. While wars and talk of them still influence our lives, my thoughts often drift back to my own childhood days, when we found ourselves the casualties of our own war.

Acknowledgments

I am grateful to my children—Kimberly, Marc, and Megan—for their continued encouragement for me to keep writing. In spite of their busy schedules, they have been helpful with the final editing of this book, and so I owe them a special thanks. Thanks also go to Seumis, my future son-in-law, whose computer expertise was of great assistance and is much appreciated.

I also owe a debt to friends for their past support and encouragement, not only in this effort but with previous other papers and articles. They are friends from my childhood with whom I had the opportunity to discuss and review several of the events described here. Special thanks to my friend Norm for his suggestions in support of this book.

Finally, a word of thanks to my mother, who still lives in Germany. She was always willing to review and talk about events I have attempted to write about. I am hopeful that this book will bring much-deserved credit to her and to the many other mothers who had to fight their own war for their families' survival.

The Early Days

My simple beginning dates back some sixty-plus years ago in a medium-sized town named Duingen located in Lower Saxony in the northern part of Germany. I was born the second son to my father, Georg, and mother Anna. Gunter, my older brother, was four years older, and after me came our younger brother, Wolfgang, and finally our sister, Marlene. My parents had given me the name Manfred, and as I recall, I have always been satisfied with that choice. Although it was a fairly common German name, it was used less frequently than many of the others they could have chosen. Our parents, together with my brother Gunter, had moved to Duingen from another part of Germany for the purpose of finding employment for Dad in the local furniture factory. Born in April 1939, I became the first in the family to be born in Lower Saxony in this town called Duingen.

Dad, a carpenter and cabinetmaker by trade, had been drafted into the German Army about the time of my birth. Coincidentally, World War II broke out just several months later. Within the early part of the war, Dad had contracted malaria and was treated at a distant hospital for a period of several months before returning to his military unit. Although he was able to come home on leave several times during those first three years, with the exception of Gunter, we were too young to remember much of those short visits. Late in 1943, Mom was advised by the war department that Dad had become a prisoner of war in Yugoslavia.

Mom had already been taking care of us by herself since Dad had been drafted some four years earlier, as was the case with most families in town and elsewhere. She was a petite five foot one or two, but for us children she always appeared much taller and stronger. When the circumstances required, she would not hesitate to reach for the wooden spoon to confirm her authority. All four of us children had inherited her dark brown hair and eyes. Gunter, the oldest, was nearly nine, and besides going to school, he had to help Mom wherever needed. He would often be required to push our sister, Marlene, in her baby buggy while Wolfgang, not quite three yet, would walk along holding onto the handlebar. I usually trailed a few feet behind them. German moms had this belief that children needed to spend time outside for fresh air regardless of the temperature. This also allowed Mom the necessary break to do her cleaning and cooking until we returned.

I recall Gunter having to take on many of these duties, including helping stack wood for year-round use or helping in the garden, in addition to help looking after us. He never grumbled about it. Wolfgang, still being under the age of three, could not be away from Mom for too long before he would begin to cry and begin calling for her. He seemed to require more attention than the rest of us and so he would spend much more time on her lap or being carried. Marlene, on the other hand, being the youngest, was nearly one by now and was quick and independent, and so she had to be supervised at all times.

The house we shared with another family bordered on to the Hauptstrasse, the German description for Main Street, and was located near the center of town. From our kitchen window, we could look directly at the neighboring gray stone factory wall only about six feet away. The kitchen and our small living room were separated by a sliding door. Each of the two rooms was only about nine by eleven feet, but keeping the sliding door open gave them a somewhat larger affect. From our living room window, we were able to look directly out on to the Hauptstrasse and the little grocery store across the street.

Upstairs we occupied three bedrooms. But this would soon to change. From our back door, a narrow walkway between our house and the adjacent factory wall led out on to the Hauptstrasse. The front door of the house led into a small yard we shared with neighbors across from us. From here, a wooden gate also exited on to the Hauptstrasse.

The house across the front yard was a two-story corner house which bordered on both Hauptstrasse and Zweftje, a side street near us. On the ground floor facing both streets was a shoe repair shop, and one could usually hear the faint hammering of footwear being refurbished. A pleasant odor of leather and glue always permeated the area near the little shop. Most of the townspeople worked in local factories and were able to walk home for their noon meal. From this typical German punctuality of people's daily movements, I learned to determine the time of day even before our little church bell would confirm it. As a young boy, I experienced this as a way of order and harmony that provided a welcoming sense of peace during those uneasy times.

Our town was larger than most of the others around us. Its design was typical of most German towns. Farms and factories were also located inside the town limits and so it created a tight community. Farmland and forests were located outside the village and began immediately beyond the last building leaving town. The odor of farm animals and manure was ever present and was accepted as part of living in a town-type community. While approaching our village from any direction, one would first see the three tall factory chimneys towering high above all other buildings. Next was the pointed steeple of our sixteenth-century Protestant church, the only church in our community. Hauptstrasse ran north to south, with Triftstrasse entering from the west, forming a T at the center of town.

As children, we were told about a long-held legend of a previous town referred to as Old Duingen. It was supposed to have been located inside the adjacent forest and about a mile from the present town. According to the legend, the town had sunken into the ground and had disappeared from sight with all its inhabitants. It was believed that children who were born on a Sunday would be able to hear the ringing of the bells from the sunken church on Easter mornings. No matter how often we walked the road passing through the forest, as we came near the assumed location of the sunken town, someone would reverently whisper, "Old Duingen" while pointing in that general direction. We all had our own thoughts about this mysterious place; however, no one ever expressed disbelief about this long-held legend.

Several of the older townspeople occasionally told us of other legends that they claimed took place there or nearby. These were people who had lived there all their lives, and hearing them in our vanishing local dialect made it most convincing to us. Oh, how we clung to these legends of times past. The town's narrow streets with its centuries-old buildings allowed us to easily transport our imagination into these legends and stories. Our medieval church with its thousand-year-old tower and attached ancient graveyard seemed a natural source for inspired and scary stories. The tower had once served as refuge for a much smaller community during attacks by outside barbarians and so it was of historical importance to the community.

Now it served as bell tower, although the brass bells had been taken out and the material used for the much-needed war effort, and a smaller single bell had taken their place. Often the bodies of those in town who had died were stored on the ground floor inside the tower for the required three-day holdover until their burial.

The attached graveyard at the back of the church was filled with headstones, some dating back to the time of the Reformation during the sixteenth century. Although the entire scene had a peaceful appearance, for us children this could easily transform into a place where ghosts roamed, especially so during the hours of darkness.

There were also many superstitions that had been passed down from previous generations and were still being taken seriously by many of the locals. Some of these nearly bordered on witchcraft and appeared quite scary for our young, trusting minds. Several of the older women had reputations for their ability to do strange and magical things. Since it was customary for older women to dress in black clothing, it was easy for us to view them as possible witches, and so we tried to maintain a safe distance from them. In spite of our negative views about these women, adults often employed their magic for the healing of warts, for example, something nearly everybody was plagued with.

To perform their healing ritual, one of these women would often take the afflicted child or adult into a room. Here she would seal off the key holes, and while a funeral procession was passing by outside, she would rinse the hand of the afflicted person with water. Warts that had been there for months or even years would then usually be gone within days. The fact that it seemed acceptable to the adult only validated this mysterious practice for us and added to our impressionable childhood imaginations.

As a result of a special clay found outside the village, Duingen had been known for its quality pottery making for hundreds of years. The old men often talked about how the trade had been passed on from one generation to the next, and nearly every second house had at one time been a small pottery shop. Occasionally we could still watch how pottery was made on individual pottery wheels driven by a craftsman's foot while his hands skillfully formed the spinning clay into individual masterpieces. Once completed and fired in special stone ovens, the items turned from their light gray color to a shiny dark brown.

For us children these were just simple pots of little significance. Our town historian would proudly tell us about the old days when these products were delivered by horse and wagon throughout Germany and even to faraway places such as St. Petersburg, Russia, a journey that would take nearly a year to complete. This was the part that I found fascinating and was always eager to hear more about.

By this time there were only a few people who still carried on this rapidly vanishing trade. The special clay was now mainly used by our two local factories for the manufacture of specially-burned drainage pipes and so remained one of the major sources of employment. The smaller of these two factories was located right next door and so we became quite familiar with the noises and the activities associated with this place. From our backyard we could look through a soot-covered window inside the dimly lit facility and see the semi-dark and crude passageways between the burning brick ovens. To us they seemed like a maze and always presented a temptation to play hide-and-go-seek, although we were rarely allowed to go inside. The burning stone ovens inside created a great deal of heat, so the workers would often just sit outside to cool down. By seeing them on a daily basis, we soon came to know each of the workers by name.

Just a short distance from our house was our small railroad station. It was operated by a private rail system that connected to the national rail system (*Reichsbahn*) about twelve miles away. The local rail system covered every little town along the way and so was a major source of transportation for those living along its line. The soot-filled smoke from the small steam locomotive often permeated the air, and from that one could quickly tell whether the train was currently in the small station. A short burst of the whistle was usually the signal that the train was either arriving or about to leave.

Weekdays, punctually at twelve noon, each of our three factories would signal with a short burst of its steam whistle and its workers would break for their noon meal. This was repeated once the break period was over and again at quitting time. All of these sounds and smells became so much part of our daily life and routine that they became part of us and unique to our community.

* * *

The war was now in its fourth year and survival became ever more difficult. By late 1943, the bombing raids on nearby cities intensified. The fire alarm located directly next to us was used to alert the community of potential air raids by sounding one long, uninterrupted alarm.

These then became frantic moments for everybody in town. They meant that bombers were already en route and could be expected over our area within ten to fifteen minutes. If the alarm was sounded when school was in session, children were quickly dismissed and sent home, running most of the way. It was necessary for each family to find some form of shelter or cover, since official bomb shelters did not exist in most towns. For us, that meant our above-the-ground potato cellar. It had strong walls but would offer no protection for a direct or nearby hit. For others, a bomb shelter was simply their basements or finding shelter with someone near their homes.

We were surrounded by several large industrial cities that were the usual targets for the frequent bombings. It was unknown, however, which of these cities would be targeted when, and so we sought shelter each and every time the air raid was sounded. During the air raids at daytime, we occasionally dared to look at the sky as the heavily-laden bombers flew overhead in what seemed to us an endless number of planes. The roaring sound of their engines became so well known to us that it transferred into an instant response of fear. Just minutes after passing overhead, we would hear and feel the impacts of the explosions as bombs were being dropped on cities only miles away.

Although the townspeople had soon recognized that the intended targets were mainly the cities, there were several local factories that could also become potential targets for destruction. Occasionally bombers on their return flights disposed of bombs that had failed to eject from their cargo holds for whatever reason. These then were dropped indiscriminately along their return route, and this made us potential targets as well.

It was most frightening during the night hours. As the siren began to sound its loud alarm next door, Mom would quickly get us out of bed and into our prepared clothing. Gunter then quickly carried our younger sister while holding the hand of Wolfgang. I ran behind on our way across the narrow yard to our potato cellar. Mom would be the last, nearly double timing while carrying her two large suitcases filled with our most needed belongings. The haste, combined with the darkness, somehow intensified the fear we all felt.

The low wooden door to our cellar would be shut and soon we would again hear the familiar sound of the approaching bombers. The dim candlelight was quickly extinguished, as we had been trained to do, and so we waited in darkness. We could feel Mom's arms tightening around us and usually very little was said. Soon we would hear the exploding bombs in the distance and feel the ground vibrating from the massive explosions. It would be several minutes before the planes returned, now on their way home. These were tense moments as we waited in the darkness of our shelter, wondering whether we would become an unscheduled target.

Although I was only about five years old, I had come to realize that, if attacked, we could easily perish inside this make-believe shelter. Perhaps I had overheard this from previous discussions among the adults. This thought would usually overtake me during these fearful moments, and yet feeling Mom's arms around me and knowing that my family was here with me was comforting. Even if we were to die, it was going to be as a family. That was often my own thought, something I never expressed verbally. It was not until the aircraft engine sounds began to fade that Mom's arms began to relax, a sign for us that it was over once again.

Soon we would hear the voices of others as people began to reappear from their makeshift shelters, now wondering which city had been hit this time. In the darkness of the night, the adults could usually determine the direction of the destruction by the illumination of the sky over the burning city. It was reassuring for us to hear these familiar voices after such frightening events, and it helped us to return to some normalcy. The stillness of the night had returned, and as I looked briefly at the stars above, I began to regain a feeling of constancy and peace, and soon we would all be back in our warm beds.

In late 1943, Marlene was being baptized in the nearby city of Alfeld. In spite of the difficulty traveling, Aunt Mary, who had come from the nearby city of Hannover, had come to be the godmother for this event. For this she had brought her two young daughters, our cousins Helga and Brigitte, age five and three respectively. Uncle Al, her husband, was away fighting at some faraway front. While visiting with us, she received notice that her house in the city had just been destroyed during a recent bomb raid, and so my aunt and my cousins had become homeless like so many others.

Unable to return home, they were now in urgent need of a place to stay. After some quick readjustments by all, two rooms were prepared for them and they began to live with us in the same house. For Mom it meant that there was now another adult person with whom she could share her fears and worries. I recall their bonding during this time of uncertainty, as they worked and supported each other in their daily struggle for survival.

I liked Aunt Mary right from the start. She talked a lot yet her voice seemed to convey so much energy and the expression of her High German pronunciation clearly distinguished her from the dialect and the slower pace of the local townspeople. She had experienced many air raids while living in the big city and so had firsthand knowledge of the actual destruction it had caused. Just prior to each attack, they would run to the nearest air-raid shelter both night and day while worrying about what might be left standing once they exited from there.

She told her stories with such vitality that we were just drawn in by them. Knowing her firsthand experiences somehow helped us feel more secure, or perhaps it was just having another adult around us. For us children it also meant that we now had two additional cousins as playmates. Our evenings became a time to be together, as we shared, played, and even laughed. And it wasn't long before we realized how blessed we were to have them live with us.

In addition to the many people seeking shelter and housing from bombed-out cities, refugees from Russian-occupied German territories were now arriving everywhere, including in our own town. I recall their frequent arrivals, usually standing on the back of open trucks or farm wagons, holding on to their meager belongings. These usually consisted of a worn suitcase, often held together with a rope, or a tied-up cardboard box. The sadness in their faces reflected the stress of their long journeys after having lost everything except what was contained in those single pieces of luggage. Young children would usually cling to their mothers, who worried about being separated from them and their meager belongings.

I was especially affected by a young girl who was standing motionless next to her mother before exiting the back of the tractor trailer on which they had arrived with several other families. Like most girls, she wore her hair in pigtails. She had briefly looked down at me from the back of the trailer, without ever changing her serious, almost painful expression. I wondered whether she really looked at me. Or was I just another object of something new and frightening on their long unknown journey? This brief contact would be forever imprinted into my memory, and I began to feel a new sympathy for these new arrivals.

After the people had been helped off the vehicles, a white delousing powder was pumped inside their clothing, which was understandably a very degrading ordeal for many of them, perhaps especially so for the women. Occasionally someone was met by a local relative and the reunion was usually an emotional event when those involved simply forgot the others around them. Even at my young age, seeing the enormous joy of people being reunited under such devastating circumstances touched me deeply, to the point of dealing with my own tears.

Others who had no one to meet them were taken to a nearby dance and exercise hall to be fed and given a temporary place to rest until available rooms could be found either in town or in one of the neighboring communities. Many of these arrivals had only the clothing they had worn for weeks during their long travel, and so the local people often referred to them in a somewhat negative way by calling them *Fluechtlinge* (refugees), which differentiated them from the locals. Although this rudeness disturbed me even at my young age, I usually remained quiet and so often felt guilty for not speaking out.

Grandma, Dad's mother, who had also been driven from her home, had been relocated at a distant town, and so arrangements were made for her to come and live with us. It was from her many stories that we began to realize what these refugees had endured under the Russian occupation before they were driven out. We learned that the journeys from their home towns to their final destination often took weeks and numerous means of transportation until they could either be placed with relatives or a place for them could be found. Shortly after Grandma's arrival, a young cousin, the daughter of one of Mom's older sisters, came to live with us as well. And so the small house became filled with family.

In spite of all that was happening, we didn't fully appreciate how fortunate we were that we could still grow some of our own potatoes. By helping local farmers with their harvest, we were sometimes able to obtain some extra potatoes. Because of this, potatoes with some gravy made from water and a little flour became our daily meals. Since there was never enough food, it required all of us to help by gleaning emptied fields for leftover potatoes or corn to be ground into flour, something city people were unable to do.

Some of the local farmers were assigned Russian prisoners to be used as cheap laborers. Although they were prisoners of war, they were free to move around town, as this was also necessary to do their work both on the farm and in the fields. For us children, we enjoyed listening as they spoke German with their hard Russian accent. Occasionally, while milking the farmers' cows, these prisoners would risk giving us boys some of the fresh milk, without the farmers' knowledge of course. Because of this kindness, it was hard for us then to think of them as our enemy—these men who, out of compassion, helped us in this small but not forgotten manner.

By fall 1944, we still had not received mail from Dad, but we would often talk about him, especially at dinnertime. Often, while listening to the adults, we could hear them discussing the course of the war, as the Allies were now pushing ahead. By now most of the surrounding cities lay in ruin, but the daily bombings still continued. The adults often discussed how they wished for all of this to be over soon.

Many now expressed their concern about which of the Allied forces might occupy our area at war's end. Refugees who had come from the already occupied Russian territories each had their own frightening stories of treatment they had received from their occupiers. Their fear of having to experience this spilled over unto the local population.

By now people were quietly speculating that Germany was definitely going to lose the war. From listening to Mom and Aunt Mary, it didn't seemed to matter anymore, as it had brought such misery for so many years. Since they were usually our major source of such input, it was natural for us children to internalize their feelings as our own. Their only hope now was that we would be occupied by either American or British troops, but only time would tell.

The fear of a Russian occupation was now more and more shared by all those in town. In my young mind, I began to wonder what an occupation would be like, especially after having heard so much about it from the refugees. Would we be hurt or possibly separated from each other, as so many had told us about? I was hesitant to ask Mom or Aunt Mary, as I realized that they too were concerned, so I kept my fears to myself.

* * *

I was expected to start my first school year in April of 1945, the following year. With the war still going on and with the uncertain future, it was impossible to predict when this was going to happen. It was not something we children were greatly concerned about then. We were quite content to just get together with other neighborhood boys, and did so at every opportunity. Gunter and a few of his friends were older, but they usually allowed us younger kids to do things with them. Being the youngest, we were easily influenced and didn't mind being used as gophers. Wolfgang was just about four by this time, and Marlene had turned two. Due to her eagerness to explore and how quick she was getting around, she needed to be watched at all times, and so she became everybody's concern.

Our family was Catholic, clearly one of the first in an all-Protestant community. As more Catholic refugees arrived from other predominantly Catholic areas, so came the need for regular Sunday services. The only church in town was of Protestant denomination; however, we were allowed to use their facility for the occasional Sunday mass. Since our Catholic community was still too small, a priest from a nearby city would come to hold an occasional service. Out of this small but growing Catholic minority, we developed a bonding that carried over into much of our social life and expanded our circle of friends. With the number of Catholics on the increase due to the arriving refugees, we were ultimately assigned our own priest, who took on the enormous responsibility of serving twelve local towns. Father Bach was a man truly devoted to his calling and so had all our affection. Each Sunday, he traveled miles on his bicycle to hold mass in at least two of the twelve towns under his care, regardless of the weather conditions.

Gunter had become one of the first altar boys and later trained me for this honorable service. We became quite proficient in rattling off the required Latin without ever understanding any of its meaning. Mom involved herself from the very beginning and did whatever was required to help our small congregation grow and survive. Often Fr. Bach would have breakfast at our house before bicycling on to the next town. Without realizing it and by necessity, we had become one of the founders and supporters of our growing Catholic community. Although this became an important part of our young lives, I often felt somewhat embarrassed while serving as an altar boy during the occasional procession through a mostly Protestant town. I couldn't help but feel that we were the odd ones simply by being the minority, and yet there never really existed any rivalry or reason for my feelings. Even among friends, the difference in religion rarely ever became an issue, and yet I couldn't shed this feeling.

* * *

I often listened in on the conversation of the adults, mostly without them realizing it. It was not intended as snooping. I wanted to hear their feelings about our situation. During one such occasion, I overheard them talk about a new unknown threat that they called the atomic bomb. Just one such device was able to kill thousands of people.

Although we had lived with the frequent bombing raids for many months, I had always feared them mostly at night. In my young mind, I had the recurring nightmare of a dark, approaching enemy whose faces I could never make out in the darkness of the night. The unrecognizable enemy would come rushing toward us and simply overrun us. I don't recall ever finishing this experience beyond that point to see the actual outcome. Fear would cause me to wake up, and so this final scene remained in my memory. I somehow associated this recurring nightmare with what I envisioned the takeover of our town would possibly be like, and I hoped it would occur during the daytime hours. Perhaps I had seen these aggressive shadows somewhere on one of the war posters and during the darkness of the night, it began to haunt me.

While lying in bed that night, with the room in total darkness, fear of this new and powerful bomb took hold of me. I wished that for once I had not tried to listen in on the adult conversation. I recall being so overcome with fear that I began to cry uncontrollably. Mom, who had heard me, hurried upstairs and came into the bedroom, asking me why I was crying. She turned on the light and sat down on my bed. Still recovering from my ordeal, I was finally able to get out the words, "Atomic bomb," and while holding me she assured me that I did not need to worry about it and that everything would be all right. It took some time for me to calm down, and Mom stayed with me until she felt that I was able to sleep. I laid there for some time with the lights on until I was finally able to fall asleep.

* * *

We often talked about Papa, referring to our Dad. We traditionally prayed for his safety before our Sunday dinner. The idea of being a prisoner of war was not something we as children fully understood. Mom always talked about him being held in some faraway country and that someday he would be coming home again. That assurance helped us to accept his absence. Late summer in 1944, we finally knew that Dad was still alive. We received a first letter from Dad. While sitting at the kitchen table at mealtime, we would look at the letter again, as if to assure that it was real. Mom then retrieved her photo album with pictures of earlier times, and it was from them that we came to know what he looked like. Gunter, being four years older than myself, could recall when Dad was still at home before going to war.

Grandma would often tell stories of Dad's childhood days. We had heard the same stories over and over again but we never seemed to tire of them. From his pictures and Grandma's stories, we tried to create an image of Dad in our minds and looked forward to the day when he would finally return home.

We were not alone in this but felt more fortunate than our neighbors across the yard. They had been advised that their dad was missing in action, news that usually left little hope for the family. Neighbors to our other side were also advised that their father had become a prisoner of war somewhere in Russia. Most our friends were in similar situations, and so we did not view the absence of our father as unique to us. Other families received the most feared news about the death of their husbands, fathers, or sons, and so they began to wear the black armband as a sign of their mourning. This usually caused me to think about what it must feel like to have a loved one buried in some faraway country—to never be able to visit their grave, as was so customary in our community.

Often out of desperation, the wives of those missing in action sought answers through the magical powers of the few old women mentioned earlier. Once seated, the old woman extracted a long hair from the inquiring wife or mother. She would then take the golden wedding ring and feed one end of the thin hair through the ring. While holding both ends of the hair between her fingertips, the ring would hang freely, supported only by the hair. While staring at the dangling ring, she would add her magic, which was usually done in silence or through her own words. The ring was now expected to give the answer by its movement. A spinning or rotation would indicate that the husband or son was no longer alive. If, however, the ring began a sort of erratic vibrating movement without turning, this was an indication that the person was still alive.

I sometimes overheard Mom mentioning the name of a woman whom she had consulted in this manner and now had an answer. She seemed serious when she talked about these matters, and I wondered about whether she actually believed in them. Following this, she usually pointed out that it was sinful for us Catholics to engage in this type of activity.

* * *

On an early fall evening, when it was still daylight outside, I had just finished supper, but for some reason I was the only person left in the kitchen. The early evening sunlight reflected off the adjacent factory wall and, from the kitchen window, created a peaceful scene. I had just gotten up from my chair and was heading for the kitchen door to go outside when suddenly the house was shaken by what seemed like an enormous explosion. Dishes rattled inside the cabinet and one of the top doors flew open. I was gripped by an instant panic, wondering whether the Russians were attacking or—even worse—if the atomic bomb had gone off. I ran to the door in fear and shouted, "The Russians are coming!" But the house stopped trembling.

Once outside, I found everybody in dismay and wondering what had just occurred. Being among familiar neighbors helped me calm down. Speculations were running rampant among the people. We had experienced many air raids in the past, but this was a totally new occurrence. Were we now under attack? Was it possible that the atomic bomb had been used? I kept asking these questions, only to have the adults stare at me. "How far away are the Russians?" seemed to be more their concern. Finally, a short time later, the news began to circulate that an underground ammunition factory in Godenau, a town about five miles from us, had exploded. People were surprised by this news, as nobody had ever expected the existence of an underground ammunition factory so near to us. But having an answer to the cause of this extraordinary event helped us at least eliminate the fear of the other possibilities.

During the early months of 1945, it became clear that the war would be lost; however, it gave us hope that it would finally be over soon. Occasionally there still appeared enemy fighter planes that frequently attacked our independent railroad. Traveling was now even more dangerous and often delayed the arrival of our daily milk ration, which was carried by train from a distant town dairy. People continued to arrive on foot, often covered in dirt from the nearby bombed-out cities. In hope of finding a place to stay, they had made this long journey on foot while pulling their little wagons, which held all their leftover possessions. Families, including those who owned their houses, were now controlled by town ordinances, and so rooms were strictly allocated depending on the number in each household. This, however, did not always have the sympathy of those who had to give up more of their precious living space.

In spite of the difficult times, we as children could often turn simple chores into fun-filled activities. By getting together with neighborhood friends, our young imaginations allowed us to escape into our own world. Although this would occasionally create rivalries with other groups, this consisted more of talk than action. With our limited resources, we developed an expertise in making and using slingshots, an activity we practiced very competitively. Sparrows were considered a nuisance back then and so became fair game for our target practice.

Loitering on the nearby farm became one of our favorite pastimes. Although we were probably a nuisance most of the time, we were usually tolerated by the farmers and their help. Even at our young age, we became quite proficient at handling a team of horses, and so we often became useful to the farmers as a source of cheap labor.

The farm offered many interesting activities for our young minds. Being around the many domestic farm animals helped us to become quite comfortable with them. Being able to lead a large workhorse by its rein made us feel somewhat superior. We found the hay lofts especially well-suited for creating tunnels, which could often occupy us for an entire afternoon.

Occasionally we would be given the task of leading a herd of cows to a pasture outside of town for a few hours of grazing. We found that it gave us a feeling of responsibility and control because we kept the herd safe, and we had fun doing it. Through this activity, we learned from the older boys in the group how to handle the herd, and it created a strong bond between us. Usually by late afternoon, after several hours of grazing, we led the herd back home. Once the animals were securely back in their stables, we were each handed a sandwich as our official pay. This was something we looked forward to and truly appreciated during those difficult days of always being hungry. Although Mom did what she could to keep us four kids fed, rationing always held this to a minimum. Having the additional source of an occasional meal was therefore always welcomed. It was during those hard times that we came to realize how much we depended on our farmers to keep us fed, and so they became well respected for it.

It seemed then that using your real first name was something reserved for the adults or special occasions. Most of us boys used nicknames, as if too embarrassed to call each other by our real names.

Instead of Manfred, my older brother Gunter used to call me Mommet, and so by his use of this nickname I became known as Mommet to the boys. Gunter, on the other hand, was called Gunner instead, and with the exception of very few of our friends, these names remained with us. Rudie became my best friend. He lived next door and was the same age as myself. His brother Juergen was only one year older but was much taller than most of the boys. Since we lived so close to each other, we were usually the first to arrive at our daily meeting at the corner shoe shop of the Hauptstrasse and Zweftje, as it was simply named without the word strasse (street) to follow.

One by one, others would join the group as we continued to linger there. Heinz, from up the Zweftje, one of the tallest boys in the group, would first check the bottoms of his sandals several times immediately after arriving. It was never clear to us what he was looking for while doing this check. The older boys, Gunter being among them, automatically took the lead and decided what, if anything, we were going to do. Just coming together on the daily basis without any real plans or purpose was something all of us looked forward to. Here we discussed and rehashed much of what we heard from the adults about the war or any of the local problems. It was also a place from which we could quickly return home, should that become necessary.

Often after supper, all seven children in the house met to play in our L-shaped hallway. It was usually already dark, but to be sure, one person would be blindfolded and then try to touch any one of the others. The first person caught would then become the next to be blindfolded, and so the game continued. This simple game would entertain us until we were asked to quit by one of the moms in the house. The darkness of the evening would usually bring with it an unexplainable anxiety or even fear for me, and so our simple play was always a welcomed diversion.

Telling frightening stories in the dark was also very effective and liked by all the children in the house. However, it was difficult to come up with new and untold stories, so the same stories would usually be told over and over again. I often became the selected storyteller and had to use my imagination to create new and frightening stories and expressions. By using a special emphasis in my voice or just whispering, there was usually absolute silence in that dark hallway. As I neared

17

the ending and the scariest part of my stories, I sensed their tensed anticipation as their breathing changed and as the younger ones tried to move up close to someone as protector. This was the time when I slowly raised my voice from a mere whisper, until I finally blurted out the frightening ending and everybody would scream in fear and delight. But they always asked for more.

One such scary story, we had been told, took place in our house in one of the upstairs bedrooms many years earlier. During the midnight hour, a knock was heard at the bedroom door. When the person inside hesitantly opened the door, he or she saw a skeleton standing there and immediately dropped dead from the shock. Repeating this story always had the affect of us becoming so scared that we could hardly breathe or move in our dark hallway. By simply mentioning in a near whisper that it happened just up the stairs made the situation almost too frightening and caused the younger among us to desperately cling to an older sibling. To further heighten the intensity of this game, I began to make low, muffled noises until finally, while raising my voice, I let out the most fierce sound I could create. This always had the expected affect, as it sent the girls screaming to the kitchen for light and safety. This exercise never lost its effectiveness, nor did we ever get tired of this silly game.

There was no toilet in our house then, so we had to go across our front yard to the outhouse attached to the stables on the ground floor of the adjacent house. The door of the toilet opened directly into the front yard, and through a round opening in the upper half of the door, one could easily inquire whether it was occupied before trying to enter. Since this needed place could not be heated, visits were held to a minimum, especially during the cold winter months. This became compounded during the hours of darkness, as the small facility had no electric light. It helped if one preplanned a visit during late daylight hours.

Our house had a small washroom equipped with two large kettles for boiling and washing clothes. Our weekly baths were taken in the kitchen next to the wood-fired kitchen stove. This occurred each Saturday evening by use of a portable bathtub. The youngest would be the first and then would be put to bed so the next could take his turn. To give the bathing person privacy, other family members remained in the small adjacent living room. The feeling of the warmth from the nearby wood-fired stove and smelling the fragrance of the soap while sitting in the tub made the experience a pleasant one, even for us children.

On Sunday morning, we prepared for attending church service. This was a time when we each tried to look our best, whatever that may have been. Our opinions were usually different from Mom's, and so it was not without tears that we sometimes made it to church on time. As clothing was also allotted on rations, Mom would make much of our clothing on her foot-pedaled sewing machine. From the yarn ration, she would knit long woolen stockings for use during the winter months. While sitting in church, the harsh wool would begin to itch our legs during the service, and I looked forward to removing them immediately after getting home. It is surprising that this small and insignificant incident has remained so clearly in my mind.

Sunday dinners were always special, as Mom would try to prepare a complete meal consisting of soup, potatoes, and gravy with some meat, and ending with dessert from her homemade canned supply. It was also a time when we tried to remember Dad, still being held as prisoner of war. We would again look at our album as our main means of trying to visualize him. Besides the preparation of the meals and the washing of dishes, no other work was performed on this day. At two o'clock in the afternoon, we listened to the children's story time on the radio, something we looked forward to all week.

* * *

It was now early 1945 and it seemed certain that the war was nearing its end. Rations were even more difficult to get and refugees were still arriving from bombed-out cities and other parts of Germany in hope of finding someplace to stay. One April afternoon, something unusual happened. Suddenly a single rider on horseback appeared. Following him at some distance was what seemed to be an endless herd of horses coming around the gradual bend of the Hauptstrasse from the north. The herd continued to pass by for minutes, heading south to an unknown destination. The rear was followed by several other riders who kept urging the herd with hand motions and by swinging ropes. It was the enormous number of horses that made this event an unusual one for us that day.

Later it was rumored that the herd of some two hundred horses had recently been bombed out of their stables in the city of Hannover and was now driven to some safe ground ahead of the approaching Allied troops. The rumors also stated that the horses had been the famous Lipizzaners; however, that was never confirmed. Their hurry seemed to indicate, however, the expectancy that the Allied troops were now rapidly approaching our area.

Each spring around this time in late April, Mom, Gunter, and sometimes Aunt Mary would spend days turning over the garden spade by spade. Although I was still too young for this hard work, I was usually allowed to rake the turned-over ground after them. Wolfgang and Marlene were of course with us and needed to be looked after as well. Once the garden had been turned over, it was time to plant potatoes one at a time and where all of us could help. Mom also planted various vegetables in perfect rows. Because of the required precision, it was something she usually preferred to do herself.

The daily bomb raids had now diminished and we took that as another sign for the war ending shortly. I had been scheduled to be admitted to the hospital in the nearby city of Hildesheim for a ruptured navel cord, something I had since birth. We had heard much about the damage this city as well as the others had suffered as a result of the constant bombings. So far the hospital had received only minor damage and was still standing. Travel and being in the city was simply too dangerous, and so my admission kept getting delayed until some future date. Enemy fighter planes still made occasional attacks on our local train and forced its occupants to run into the open fields to avoid being shot at.

During one such attack, a fighter plane crashed between our town and the neighboring town. The pilot had ejected and landed safely in one of the nearby fields. A local farmer, who had lost a son in the war, was the first to spot him as he was parachuting to the ground. In his fury, he began to chase the young pilot with his pitchfork in hand while shouting his threats. Others nearby recognized the farmer's intention and intervened before he could reach the downed pilot and do him harm. Being greatly outnumbered, the young pilot then allowed himself to be taken captive and taken away, probably for his own safety.

The following day, a group of us boys went out to the described location, where the plane had crashed. On our way there, we had discussions of what we might find of the downed plane. To our disappointment, only a few small fragments of the plane's wings and body had remained scattered over a large area. We were told that, since the plane had a machine gun and ammunition on board, it would have been dangerous for scavengers such as us to find those things, so they had previously been removed.

The bombing had now stopped and rumors circulated about what this could mean for us. We knew that Allied troops were coming closer each day, and there was no preparation to offer any kind of resistance by those in town. We often talked among ourselves about what it would be like when it was finally over. We had lived with this war ever since I could remember. So many refugees had come here over the past years that the population of our town had nearly doubled. We were slowly gaining new friends of families who had moved near to us. Although we would at times draw a distinction between the locals and the refugees, in reality we were all basically poor and struggling to survive, so any difference soon faded.

It didn't seem to matter anymore who won or lost the war, as long as it was over and done with. I wondered if this was simply the thinking of the women and the old and whether those fighting cared any more about the outcome. It was a relief not to have to endure the endless bombing raids any longer. There was frequent talk about what to expect from the Allied troops when they arrived. The adults were hoping for an occupation by the Ammys, as we usually referred to American Forces. The British Forces were always referred to as Tommys, probably because Tom was known as a commonly used English name.

There was hardly a day now that we did not talk about Dad and his homecoming once the war was finally over. We were certain that the end of the war also meant an automatic release from his confinement in Yugoslavia. I tried to picture his homecoming and thought how good it would be to have a strong man to protect us. Whether he would still look like his pictures was something we often debated. How good it would be for Mom to have him help with all the hard work she had handled nearly all by herself all these years. All these and other thoughts kept running through my mind, but we would have to wait just a little while longer.

Day of Liberation

It was the beginning of May 1945 and I had turned six only a few days earlier. This particular day would become one most memorable for all of us in town. I clearly recall my reaction as I walked out of the house that morning and went through the gate in the yard and out onto the Hauptstrasse. My attention was immediately drawn to the white bed sheets hanging out of our attic window. As I turned to look down the street, I realized that nearly every house along our street had a white sheet hanging out of its attic window as well. I didn't have to wait long before my older brother, Gunter, explained the reason for the sheets as a sign of capitulation. I had heard the word *capitulation* used numerous times from the adults before and was aware that it meant our surrender without a fight.

While coming together with neighboring friends, we began to wonder about when all of this had occurred. "The mayor has ordered white bed sheets to be hung out of every attic window," one of the older kids informed the rest of us.

"The Ammys are coming," someone else said.

"When?" we responded in surprise, as we stared at the boy who had just said that.

"I guess soon," was all he could say, lifting his shoulders to confirm that he didn't know.

I looked up at the sky, as this was usually where we had known the danger to come from. It was overcast but peaceful. The adults had always hoped to be occupied by American troops, and now it was going to happen. It was ironic that our enemy would now become our liberators and save us from prolonged suffering. At least now we were assured that it was American and not Russian troops, as had been feared all along. Now people began to discuss what the Americans would be like and how we, as their former enemy, would be treated by them.

Although there was a quiet expectancy, it was not a feeling of fear that I sensed from observing the adults during the course of the morning. It had become the main topic of discussion for everybody. There was speculation about how soon this was going to happen, and new information circulated the town frequently. It was about four in the afternoon when information was received that American troops were now less than ten kilometers away and approaching quickly.

They were expected to come over the Ith hills from the west, and from there it would be less then three kilometers before they would arrive here. It wasn't long before we heard several shots being fired from the expected direction, and I could feel my anxiety rising with anticipation. People began to meet at the marketplace at the center of town, where the Triftstrasse met the Hauptstrasse. There didn't seem to be any panic in the people's behavior, which helped me to relax. Two older men standing near us were discussing that the shots fired were only intended to discourage any possible resistance. I couldn't help but wonder how they knew that to be the case and who was left to even consider anything like this. The only German soldiers we ever had in town were those home on leave visiting family, and even that had been some time ago.

I don't recall whether a curfew had been issued, but some of the people began to leave while others began to move away from the market square to the sidewalks, allowing them to disappear quickly if needed. Gunter and I had positioned ourselves at the entrance of a neighboring farm that faced the immediate center of town and overlooked the market square. From here we could see anything that came through town from any of the three directions. It also allowed us to quickly disappear into the farmer's yard, should this become necessary. It was now nearly five and we could see that those still waiting were nervously looking in the direction from which the troops were expected to come. From our location we could see down Triftstrasse about five hundred feet before it wound to the right and became blocked by houses bordering the street. We were talking somewhat excitedly while wondering what to expect shortly. It was difficult not to feel a certain fear when recalling the numerous air raids we had endured during the previous months.

We didn't have to wait long before we heard the approaching sound of motors, and our anxiety was now racing to its peak. There was also a clicking sound unfamiliar to us. Now the first vehicle, a jeep, appeared from behind the houses, followed by a small truck. Within just seconds, a frightening-looking tank and large truck with a gun mounted at the top made their way around the bend. We quickly realized that the unfamiliar clicking sounds were made by the metal tracks of the moving tank. As it rolled toward us, the noise of the metal tracks rolling across the cobblestone road created a frightening sound. The leading vehicle had now reached the intersection where the two streets met, and here the convoy came to a halt.

"What do Americans look like?" was the thought that raced through my head. "Would they look frightening and act mean?" was the real fear in my young mind. A soldier on the passenger side of the jeep now stepped out and held onto the vehicle with one hand. Turning back, he gave a command to the soldiers in the vehicles behind him. Immediately several of them dismounted the trucks and, with their rifles in hand, joined what seemed to be the officer in charge.

With their brown uniforms and their net-covered helmets, it was difficult to determine what to make of them. The officer in charge was without a rifle but carried a pistol in a light-brown case attached to his belt.

Without speaking, both Gunter and I watched with excitement, wondering what was going to happen next. As I looked toward the tank, the third vehicle in the convoy, I noticed the gun turret rotating from right to left as the big gun made its arc. I wondered if he was going to shoot. Looking back at the officer and the soldiers who had joined him, I noticed that two of them had slung their rifles over their shoulders, while they were now casually talking. As our attention was concentrated on this little gathering, I was now able to see what our previous enemy actually looked like. While carefully watching their movements, I sensed a certain casualness that caused much of my previous fear to gradually disappear.

While the officer and the others were still talking, our town mayor approached the small group from the market square. He was accompanied by a woman whom I recognized as one of our school teachers. "She speaks English," my brother said without taking his eyes from the group. She and the mayor were now addressing the American officer, and from our view we could see her looking at the mayor and then over at the officer and back at the mayor, obviously translating what was being said. The officer had retrieved a brown leather case from the jeep and began looking at some papers.

Other soldiers now began to dismount their vehicles. With their rifles hung from their shoulders, they casually walked to other vehicles, exchanging words and even laughs with fellow soldiers. Some of them lit cigarettes and looked quite relaxed. Any fear left in me began to diminish. "I wonder what they are going to do," I recall saying to Gunter, who just looked at me for a brief moment without giving a reply.

The officer was still speaking to the two townspeople when the mayor began pointing to the house across the street only two buildings away. The faces of the small group turned in that direction, as if to assess the situation. Without exposing our position, we were not able to see if anything was going on at the house of our family doctor, which was only a few feet away. Nothing alarming had changed with the other soldiers. Some of them were casually talking with the drivers of the vehicles. "I wonder what they want at that house?" I heard my brother say as the officer in charge gave instructions to the soldiers with him. Immediately, four of them approached the house with their guns in hand, and a certain excitement began to rise within me again.

We were unable to see them entering the house, but shortly thereafter they reappeared with Mr. Hubert, who also lived in the doctor's house. As they brought him to the market square from across the street, it became clear that he had been taken prisoner. We could now see that his hands had been tied behind his back and that he was being guided to a certain location.

The small group then stopped by the telephone pole next to the concrete water-storage tank used for fire emergencies. The four soldiers who had escorted him here now positioned themselves with their rifles aimed at their prisoner at about a twenty-five-foot distance. Watching this event, I felt my heart pounding, as I was certain that we were about to witness an execution of one of our townspeople.

While watching the scene before us, I recalled how we used to refer to him as "Pickle Hubert," as he had been feared for his strict sense of duty as police officer some years back. Although he had retired from this job, he still continued to exercise a certain authority and was generally disliked for his strict behavior. Now he was standing against the pole facing four guns. The people who had dared to stay watched with anticipation of what was playing out at the market square. Not much was said between Gunter and myself as we both stared at the man by the pole. "Can they do that?" I asked. After waiting a while, "I guess they can" was the short reply I received from him.

"Can they shoot us if they see us here?" I wondered. Several minutes had passed now and I couldn't help but wonder why they had picked him. Would they kill him just because he was known as a nasty person? The other soldiers hardly paid attention to what was going on just a few feet away from them. "Maybe they do this all the time and are used to it." My mind was racing with all these questions. Suddenly the four soldiers lowered their rifles and approached Mr. Hubert at the pole. Taking him into the middle of their group, they marched him off as several other soldiers accompanied them. From our location, we were unable to see where they were taking him.

Immediately following this tense scene, an announcement was made in German through a loudspeaker that a curfew would be in effect until seven o'clock tomorrow morning. All people were to remain in their homes and off the streets. Gunter and I quickly made our way back to our house, only a short away distance by way of the farmer's yard. I continued to watch from behind the safety of the fence in our yard. Military vehicles were now beginning to roll all over town. As I gave a last look toward the center of town, I could see that a large tank had been positioned at the intersection. Its gun turret was rotating until it finally stopped with the huge gun pointing directly where I was standing at a distance of about fifty feet. Did he see me, and was he going to shoot? I quickly ran into the house and remained there for the night. We could hear the heavy tanks rolling across our cobblestone road just outside our window for most of the evening and throughout the night. The noise was heightened as it reverberated between the closely placed houses, and it resulted in the rattling of dishes inside the cabinets.

Our curiosity caused us to rise up earlier than usual the next morning. I recall looking out the window on to the Hauptstrasse. Here I could see what seemed to be an endless number of American soldiers sitting on the sidewalks, their backs against walls and buildings. Many of them were still asleep with their guns either lying across their laps or leaning against the wall beside them.

They must have arrived during the night, was our guess. As some of them were beginning to rise, I realized that many of them were black soldiers, and I recalled then that I had only seen a black person in photos. As I studied them from behind the safety of our living room window, I came to realize that they acted the same as the rest of the soldiers, and I began to question what I had expected to be different.

About mid-morning, we were aroused by a knock at the front door. When Mom opened the door she was greeted by three soldiers, who advised her in broken German that they were conducting a house-to-house search for weapons. This became our first direct contact, and it helped us to feel at ease. The information that Mr. Hubert had been arrested the previous evening had spread quickly. Rumors of several reasons for his arrest were being speculated about, and although I sensed that people knew why he was arrested, they were reluctant to say it openly. From our previous experiences with him, he commanded little sympathy from the community.

Although there were curfews placed on the local population, they only lasted for a few days. It was surprising for us that many of the soldiers recognized the shortages that existed and frequently gave us children chocolate, gum, or even a sandwich. So we became quite attached to our new liberators. We were treated well by the occupation troops, and I recall a harmonious coexistence between the military and the local population. As a young boy of six, I enjoyed watching the frequent military movements that followed and quickly began to feel quite safe under our new occupiers.

The American occupation had a tremendous impact on all of us. The generosity we experienced during those early days eliminated any negative feelings that may have existed prior to this period. Having been raised in a structured, somewhat homogeneous society, we recognized that the American soldiers' actions were far less inhibited. This was most noticeable for us in their walk and movements, which appeared as a relaxed swaying, rather than rushing for a purpose. Also, their association toward each other was much less formal yet natural. Germans called this *lassig*, something they envied but could not quite imitate. It somehow impressed me immensely, and it was during this time of occupation that my earliest desire to come to America began to flourish within me.

The American troops had made their headquarters inside the red brick office building of a local company that operated a large sand quarry just outside of town. It was also one of the most attractive buildings in town. One of the officers who frequently entered and exited this building had given me chocolate and gum on a few occasions. He was a tall and slender man, but always seemed friendly in spite of our nagging and asking for chocolate.

Occasionally I would wait outside hoping he would come out so that I could walk with him. While walking, he would try speaking a few sentences in German while usually smiling down at me. Although this simple gesture seemed insignificant, it did leave a lifelong impression on me.

The war was declared officially over just a few days after the troops occupied our town, and peace had finally arrived. The period following under the Allied occupation was full of many good childhood memories. The American troops' presence was an assurance that we had no longer to fear war or a possible takeover by Russian forces. They had become our liberators, which gave us hope for a brighter future.

A New Beginning

Now that the war was finally over, we could begin to think about living instead of just surviving each day. We were hopeful for things to improve but also realized that a recovery from such a long, devastating war would require time. The reichsmark continued to be the official currency and rationing cards remained in use. We no longer had to worry about being at war but were now feeling the devastation of a destroyed country and its economy, so times remained hard. People began to trade for things most needed, and cigarettes especially became a much sought-after commodity. They then could be traded for a pair of nylon stockings or other things difficult to obtain, and so a black market evolved. People were now more open to talk about things previously only said in a whisper, and the names of people feared in the past were now mentioned openly.

We were hopeful that Dad would be released as prisoner of war and would be coming home soon. The hope for the return of loved ones was shared by many in town. Pictures of missing loved ones were now posted everywhere in hope that someone would be able to provide information of their last known status or whereabouts. Some were now desperately hoping to find news about fathers or sons missing in action. Others were looking for family members who had been separated while hurriedly leaving occupied Russian territories. Those who had fled the cities as their homes were destroyed were usually unable to leave forwarding addresses to other family members or relatives.

Train stations had now become hopeful places, as people displayed pictures of loved ones in hope of finding an answer from someone able to make an identification. Often desperate mothers or wives stood at such busy places holding up pictures with the question, "Have you seen this man, last seen in Stalingrad?" (or at one of the many other fronts). The Red Cross became an organization that helped many in this process find answers by assisting in locating missing family members. Returning German soldiers now became an important source of help to identify comrades with whom they had served, and they occasionally provided information or closure about someone previously listed as missing in action.

As life returned to some normalcy, it was suggested by our family doctor that I undergo my long overdue navel cord operation. This required a visit to the nearby city of Hildesheim for a pre-examination at the city hospital. Although it was only about a twenty-five mile journey, it required changing trains once to get there. I had always enjoyed watching our little commuter train but now, seeing the enormous black steam locomotive of the *Reichsbahn* (national railway system) with its many uniformly shaped green passenger cars, was truly exiting. Immediately after we hurried to get on, the slamming of doors echoed through the station, and within seconds the train began to move.

As we began to approach the outskirts of the city some thirty minutes later, we were able to see the enormous destruction that had occurred here. I recall wondering what fear these people must have endured during the many bombings that took place here, and over all the other cities throughout the country. I couldn't help but think of the many mothers with their children hurrying to the nearest air-raid shelter, trying to carry with them whatever they could, as we had done so many times.

While crammed inside the dimly lit shelter, they must have felt the exploding bombs above them and hoped that their home or apartment would once again be spared. I recalled Aunt Mary often telling us about her experiences during such air raids on Hannover, and now seeing the destruction firsthand helped me to understand.

When we finally arrived at the Hildesheim *Hauptbahnhof* (main station), we noticed the numerous signs indicating the direction to the nearest air-raid shelters, something Mom explained to me as we were heading for the exit. Coming out of the underground walkways that connect the tracks to the station, we began to see the damage incurred here. Piles of rubble and bricks were everywhere and people were rushing between them. Men with picks and shovels were at work uncovering tracks, while others were pushing wheelbarrows loaded with stones and dirt. Sections of the curved roofing were either missing or distorted.

People were rushing in all directions and loudspeakers were blasting the arrival and departures of trains always beginning with "*Achtung, achtung,* on track number ..." As my first experience at such a large station combined with the business of the many people, I was simply in awe. Mom just pulled me along toward the exit without much being said by either of us.

Once outside, we came to see what seemed impossible to describe. We stopped briefly and realized that we were now in the middle of the destruction, as a city in ruin lay before us. Entire city blocks of three- and four-story brick buildings were completely destroyed. Partial walls remained standing with occasional sections of stairways still hanging from their sides, and I wondered what kept them from falling. I recall gazing at a corner wall with a partial third floor still intact. A single bed was left standing in its corner, with everything around it in ruin. These were apartments where occupants had lived peacefully not so long ago, and I wondered where all the people had gone. I now came to see the enormous destruction of the bombings we used to hear and feel from the cover of our potato cellar only months ago. Although I was only six years of age, the memories of this sight would remain with me forever.

Mom pointed out the occasional concrete entrances to air-raid shelters, a protection most towns did not have. Men and women were already at work chipping mortar off bricks and then placing them on growing piles. Since many of the remaining partial brick walls seemed to be in danger of collapsing, it was prudent to maintain a safe distance. How tempted its previous occupants must have felt to search through this dangerous rubble in hope of finding something dear to them from their past.

With the exception of several windows that were now covered with large plywood sheets, the hospital had remained intact. A nurse noticed Mom's curious look and explained that the damage to the windows had occurred from nearby explosions. Shortly after our arrival I was examined by a doctor, who confirmed that an operation was necessary and that a date would be advised within the next few weeks.

On our way back to the station, we came upon a small eating place near the station. It had previously been a stable for horses, and although the building had mostly been destroyed, a small section had remained undamaged. It had been cleaned out and now offered a few tables for its guests. The tiled walls still contained the metal rings to which the horses had previously been tied. The floor's drainage runs were further evidence of a previous use. We each had a bowl of soup, the only thing offered, before we returned to the station for our train ride home.

Several weeks following this checkup, I was admitted to the hospital and given a bed in a large room with twelve other children. One of the two windows of our room was covered with a plywood sheet, something we found to be quite normal by now. My operation was performed the following day, but I had to remain in the hospital for a week of recovery. Each night before going to sleep, one of the nuns would lead us in singing Brahms's "Lullaby," something that became very special for all of us in that room. While singing the words, it brought to mind the fearful nights we had experienced only a few months earlier and the ruins just outside our windows. As night approached, I was still bothered by the unexplainable anxiety and so singing this song together helped me to relax. Even when hearing it today, it brings to mind those evenings at our hospital room, and a feeling of peace still comes over me.

I was released about eight days later and Mom, together with a neighbor lady, came to take me home. They realized that I would not be able to walk the long distance to the station and so they shared carrying me on their back. On the way to the station, our neighbor decided to briefly look up an old relative who had lived nearby. His house had also been destroyed and he had moved into the basement of the bombed-out structure. To reach him, we had to climb over rubble and finally through an opening in the ground, down a ladder, and into his meager living quarters in the basement. I was carefully let down, so not to strain the stitches on my stomach. With the exception of a single candle and the light coming in through the opening above, it was quite dark. The furniture consisted of an iron frame bed and a small table with two old chairs. A small corner cabinet was stacked with several pots and dishes. We did not see any other rooms and so assumed that this was now his entire living space.

When I asked to use the toilet, the man pointed to a nearby metal bucket in the corner. Not only was it difficult for me to make use of this facility, but it provided absolutely no privacy. Shortly after this experience, we left for the station and home, where I had much to tell the rest of the family about my experiences of the past week.

It was late summer now and farmers were busy harvesting their crop. It was my favorite time, as I often watched horse-and-wagons going and coming from the fields. There was something about the business that I found soothing. Perhaps it was the longer days, as it stayed light until nearly nine o'clock.

American troops continued to occupy our area; however, we were free to follow our daily activities without any restrictions, and so we shared a peaceful coexistence. There was a special friendliness toward us children by our occupiers, which often resulted in receiving a piece of gum or chocolate. We had quickly learned the two English words "gum" and "chocolate" and so were able to specifically ask for them. The occupation troops also provided a sense of security that allowed people to talk openly rather than whisper the names of those previously feared. Atrocities were talked about that people had feared but had never dared to ask about before.

A Newly Found Power

From the security of the sidewalk and facing the intersection at the center of town, I enjoyed watching the daily movements of military convoys. They could be coming from any of three directions and still had to pass through this intersection. I am not sure what it was that fascinated me so much about their activity that I could easily watch them for hours on end. Perhaps it was their uniforms and the identical colors of their vehicles that set them apart as something special.

One afternoon, while I was standing at my usual spot, a small British military vehicle approached from the west and halted at the intersection. The soldier on the passenger side began to look at a road map, trying to determine whether to turn north or south. After a brief moment, he pointed north and the driver began to head in that direction. From my previous watching of convoys, I had come to realize that often additional vehicles would follow this lead vehicle at some specific interval. It wasn't long before a small convoy consisting of various types of military vehicles approached again from the west. They too came to a halt at the intersection, as the passenger in the lead vehicle began to look both north and south in confusion.

At this point, I was only about thirty feet from and the vehicle and was directly facing it. I began to point north, moving my arm quickly with my index finger extended. Almost immediately, both the driver and passenger noticed my indication and, to my surprise, began to turn in that direction with the other vehicles following.

I was quite surprised about this, and to be sure that it was my indicating that caused them to turn, I stationed myself again at the same spot during the next few days. Surprisingly, I was able to repeat this maneuver at least once more and was quite pleased with my newly found power. It wasn't long before I decided that the next time I would try to point the convoy in the opposite direction of the lead vehicle. The next group of vehicles was going to be my test case. Later that afternoon, another single vehicle appeared and ultimately turned north. The following vehicles would likely appear around the bend just a few minutes later. My excitement grew while waiting, and soon I could hear the approaching motors.

As had happened previously, they too came to a halt at the intersection and I immediately began to point south, the opposite direction of the earlier lead vehicle. At this moment the driver looked at the passenger as if to await his instructions. The passenger then nodded his head in that direction and the vehicle began to turn south with five additional vehicles following them.

Standing there somewhat surprised about my success, I realized that I had better go into hiding, as the convoy would surely realize that they had been misled. I quickly hid behind the large barn door at the adjacent farm and waited.

It was only minutes before the convoy obviously realized that they were going in the opposite direction and were now returning, heading north without stopping. Peeking through the crack in the barn door, I could see the small convoy passing through the intersection again. I waited a while before coming out of the barn I had used as my hiding place. As we often played inside this barn, I was familiar with all its hidden places and felt quite secure. Pondering about my newly discovered power, I made my way home, just a few houses away. For fear of being recognized, I waited several days before I dared to show myself again at the intersection. The temptation lurked within me to try this again, but I decided to wait until a later time, just to be safe.

* * *

The Early Post-War Period

It was now fall and time for digging up our potatoes. Each batch had to be carefully uprooted so not to damage them, and then manually picked out of the ground. This was an activity where children could be useful in collecting them, and so it became a family activity that would last for days. This was also a time when we received our ration of coal. A family friend who worked in the forest service usually received a greater portion of wood and would usually share the extra portion with us. As this was our main source used for heating and cooking, we needed to make additional trips to the nearby forest in search of additional wood for the coming winter. This was usually the job assigned to Gunter and myself.

Mom was now receiving an occasional letter from Dad, but there was no indication of his coming home soon. The days were getting shorter now and it was getting dark by six and even earlier each day. It was my least favorite time of the year and would usually remain so until the first snowfall. Prior to our evening meal, we often enjoyed a few games of hide-and-seek with the neighborhood boys, which soon turned into a daily routine for us. Planning our nightly hallway get-together for play after supper usually helped me divert my unexplainable anxiety about the earlier darkness.

Our first peacetime Christmas would be in 1945. The cabinet factory, where Dad had worked prior to being drafted into the military, had planned their first Christmas party for the families of employees. The tall pine tree at the entrance of the factory had been decorated with colored lights and gave off a very festive appearance. Blackout restrictions had made it impossible to light the tree in previous years and so we truly enjoyed this new sight. By passing through several production halls, we finally arrived where Santa Claus was scheduled to appear. While waiting, I recall the smell of the wood and glue with the added odor of varnish used in the making of cabinets, and the mixture of it all seemed like a pleasant fragrance to me.

Additional colored lights had been hung inside the hall, and they gave it a festive atmosphere. Long tables were filled with colorful wooden toys. Plates filled with cookies were set up on an adjacent table and it felt awkward to be able to help oneself. Soon Santa Claus appeared and each child was called up to receive a toy. Although the toys were rather simple in design, the event was memorable, as it indicated a new beginning.

Although Germans celebrate a first and second Christmas Day, Christmas Eve is the highlight of the season. All the children in town were usually sent to the five o'clock Protestant service as a means of getting them out of the house. The church was filled with restless children anxiously waiting for the service to be over. The annual Christmas play, as part of the service, would usually get some attention; however, as soon as it was over, the children would rush to get out and then run home filled with anticipation. The church was only a two-minute distance for us, and we usually reduced that by half on our return home.

Upon coming into the kitchen, the sliding door to the living room would be closed. "Was Santa here?" was usually the first question we all had, even though we had begun to question his existence. Mom wouldn't say, but required that we all sing "O Holy Night" together. Our anticipation became almost too much when she required that we sing the second verse as well.

After a brief pause, she would open the sliding door to the living room and there, in its glory, stood the Christmas tree with all its decoration. Burning candles had been clipped onto its branches, and the light was reflected in the bulbs and in the glitter hanging from its branches. The sight of the tree was truly the high point of the evening, and it is what I remember most vividly. After the initial "oo" and "ah," we began excitedly to look for our individual plates of cookies and nuts. Mom had usually been able to get each of us at least one present.

For me it was a hand-knit sweater, something she had done secretly at night after we had gone to bed. Once the excitement had settled down, Mom would serve her homemade potato salad and wieners, which was to become our traditional Christmas Eve meal. While eating, we remembered Dad and wondered if he was able to enjoy Christmas and whether he would be coming home during the new year.

During the winter months, there was less to do around the house and so we enjoyed sledding, provided we had snow. The Zweftje around the corner was ideal for this purpose. Just outside our school building was the starting point. The entire street consisted of a continuous incline and so once the sled started to move, it would increase in speed until it reached the bottom, where it crossed the Hauptstrasse. This was the dangerous part, as it became difficult to stop without running across this main street and into the adjacent wall. The Zweftje had two sharp turns with houses bordering directly onto the street without sidewalks. To be able to make these turns, without slowing down, became the challenge for us.

We were occasionally told not to use this street for sledding; however, it was seldom enforced. Knowing this, we usually watched for our local police officer so that we could quickly disappear from the area, should this become necessary. If caught, the sled would usually be impounded by him and parents were then notified, something we desperately tried to avoid.

Wolfgang was nearly five by now and was determined to sled down this street by himself. He had not yet learned how to steer a sled; nor did he know how to stop. So on his first try downhill, being unable to stop at the bottom of the street, he continued at full speed across the main road until he finally smashed into a telephone pole. Ending up with a bloody nose, he began to cry. By coincidence, our town doctor just happened to come by and noticed the blood. He took him along to his office just a few houses away and there took care of him. After this unpleasant experience, we allowed him to ride with us.

Sundays were normally considered a day of rest and no work was performed with the exception of those working as railroad personnel—children who were sledding. Occasionally on a winter Sunday, one of the local farmers would offer one of his horses. He allowed us to tie our sleds behind each other and form a long line of sleds that was pulled by a single horse. Other times farmers would go for a Sunday afternoon ride in their full-sized sleigh, which was usually pulled by a single horse.

Mom would always have the wood- or coal-fired kitchen stove lit, and I recall the kitchen was the most comfortable room in the house. The kitchen stove would serve numerous purposes. In addition to cooking and baking, it would heat the room, keep water and the iron hot, toast our bread, and dry the kitchen towels. Before going to bed at night, Mom would bank the fire in the stove so that it would burn very slowly but still give up warmth first thing in the morning.

* * *

A Sledding Surprise

On one such winter day, I had promised my sister (only about three then) and our two cousins that I would give them a sled ride down Zweftje. After tying two sleds together, what we called bobsleds, I had our older cousin (also about seven, like myself) sit on the front sled, which I intended to steer with hands and feet from the second sled. The younger two girls were seated behind me for safety. Only a few other children were sledding at the time, so we had the street nearly to ourselves. After a slight push with my feet, we began to move and continued to increase speed going down hill.

We had just gone through our first turn with no problem and were now approaching the second curve to the right. As we were coming around the second turn for our final straight run, we realized four women were walking down the middle of the road going downhill and so facing away from us. By now we had gained speed and were quickly approaching them from behind. They seemed to be engaged in a conversation and paid no attention to our screaming; nor did they make any effort to step aside. What was I to do?

As we were rapidly approaching the ladies, I began to dig both heels into the snow, hoping to stop, or at least to slow down. Although we reduced our speed, we were not able to stop in time. Unable to avoid them, we ran into one of the unsuspecting ladies in the back of her legs and caused her to tumble and end up seated on the front of our sled with her legs high up in the air, struggling for balance. While screaming, she was forced to remain there until I was able to bring our bobsled to a halt. She then quickly jumped off and started to beat down on me while screaming in anger. She made no effort to listen to my telling her that we had tried to warn them of our coming. After feeling the back of her legs and still shouting angrily at me, she finally let up and began to join the other woman. We just sat quietly waiting for them to disappear. While walking away from us, the injured lady kept looking back as if to assure herself that we were not behind them.

Following this, we attempted to do one more run but somehow felt discouraged from going on, so we stopped sledding for that day. By the following day, the entire neighborhood had heard of our previous sledding disaster. Recalling this event during later years usually resulted in many good laughs, especially when we tried to visualize the helpless lady riding on the front of our lead sled.

* * *

1946, A New Year

It was the new year 1946 and only very few of the prisoners of war had returned home. Dad and many others remained prisoners. Although mom was receiving an occasional letter, none of them gave us any hope for an early release. At least we knew that he was still alive, so we were better off than many other families in town. At dinnertime Mom would often tell us about the contents of the last letter from him and soon thereafter grandma would again tell us about his childhood days. He was her only child, and grandpa had died as result of the First World War, so Dad had hardly known his father. She had come from a well-to-do family and had hoped to use her inheritance for Dad's education, as she had wanted him to become a doctor. The runaway inflation of the late twenties had wiped out all hopes for such a plan.

Grandma often talked about the early days. It was obvious that she, being one of only two children, was used to an easier life. She had married Grandpa, who was considered a well-educated man in his time and had held the position of director in a small school. Although Grandpa was not wealthy, with his position came certain benefits and status. Being invited to the annual ball, hosted by the regional aristocracy, were such benefits. While telling us about this important event in her life, her face took on a certain glow, and she would slowly sway while holding up one arm in a pretend dance. For that brief moment, she relived the glamour of those earlier days, and with her head held back, she moved gracefully through the room.

While moving about in this temporary state of relived glamour, she would begin to talk in the third person. It was something we all thought of as segments of stories we had heard, but at the same time, we realized how special these events must have been for her. On those occasions when Father Bach came for breakfast at our house, she would be the first to greet him in her flamboyant manner by asking, "How is your reverence today?" Then she would follow by asking, "Would your reverence like coffee?" She treated him like a member of the aristocracy—in a manner totally out of place. He would just smile and thank her, and somehow she seemed rewarded by his simple gesture.

*   *   *

My First School Year

The new school year started immediately after the Easter vacation. We had missed the previous year due to the uncertainty of the war situation and so this would officially be our first school year. Our town only had one school building consisting of four large schoolrooms, and so classes were scheduled for half-day sessions with morning and afternoon periods. An additional room was prepared in a neighboring building to accommodate the unusually large group of this year's incoming students. The school was near the top of Zweftje and only about a five minute walk from our house. I had been inside the building once before and liked the worn student desks with their inkwells. The teacher's desk up front with the large blackboard behind demanded a certain attention. There was a certain smell I enjoyed, which was probably a mixture of ink and chalk.

For children entering their first year, it was traditional to receive a specially designed cone-shaped bag about a foot and a half in length. These were usually colorful and bright. Filled with candies or a variety of other sweets, they were called sugar bags. The newly enrolled children were allowed to bring these bags to school on their first day only. We proudly carried our specially designed backpacks, which contained a small blackboard and chalk. An eraser sponge dangled from the side of the backpack and would fly about wildly as the children ran or walked. The war had been over for nearly a year and we were still living on short rations. I wondered how Mom had been able to get the backpack and the sugar bag with its contents during these difficult times.

After the initial day, we soon began to settle in and I found school quite enjoyable. I would usually meet my friend Rudie from next door, and we walked the short distance to school and back daily. Since our startup had been delayed by one year, there were in fact two age groups entering the same year, so our class had been split into an A and B class. Since Rudie and I were in the B class, our sessions were held in the afternoon.

Our first-year teacher was Ms. Heimlich, who was probably in her mid-fifties. Due to her graying hair, she seemed quite old by our estimation. She was bowlegged and as she walked her body would sway from side to side with each step. She was also a Catholic, and since there were very few of us who were Catholic in this predominantly Protestant community, we were drawn together by this religious bond. This often required her to have contact with Mom. The fact that our grandfather had been a director of a small school formed an additional bond between her and my grandmother, who was now living with us. I considered these facts to be assets, to be drawn upon when needed, and this was soon put to the test.

As she administered punishment, often for the smallest of reasons, having this family connection would surely be to my advantage. Even though we were only first graders, she would usually not hesitate to use her whip across our open hands. If one pulled away while she tried to administer this type of punishment, it would automatically be doubled.

Sometimes she would command the unfortunate one to lean over his or her desk, and then she would hit him or her across the rear. Even though it was frightening and painful, it was considered a standard disciplinary action and fully acceptable by most parents. One would usually not even mention this to a parent for fear of receiving an additional punishment, as teachers could not be wrong.

We were by now several months into the first school year, and with the occasional stern voice calling me to pay attention, things were going along quite well. Summer vacation was only six weeks long, so by mid August school was back in full session. It was the beginning of harvest time and it was difficult for me to concentrate on school activity. I was yearning to be outside. It must have been during one of those moments that Ms. Heimlich had called on me and I just did not respond in time. I hadn't even noticed her coming closer to my desk, when suddenly her hand hit me across the face so unexpectedly that I jumped up in surprise. It all had happened so quickly that I was momentarily stunned. Instead of shouting at me, as she would usually have done, she began to step back, staring at my face with a surprised expression. All the children had now turned and were staring in my direction. One of the girls, just a seat away, looked at me in shock and, while placing her hand over her mouth, pointed at me while turning her face to the teacher. Others were now doing the same, as I was still recovering from my initial shock. I realized that the teacher's face had quickly changed from that of anger to a look of panic.

As I brought my hand up to my stinging face, I realized that warm blood was gushing from my nose down my chin and onto my shirt and trousers. I was then nervously instructed to sit down and to lean my head backwards. Ms. Heimlich then stepped toward me, while at the same time she ordered one of the children to quickly bring her the cloth from the blackboard. In an instant, her anger had turned into total concern as she placed the cloth over my nose. From my leaned back position, I tried to see the other children, who had quickly gathered around and were all staring down at me. In spite of my hurting nose and my bloody condition, it was quite enjoyable to be the center of all this attention.

Although I had just received a punishment, I felt quite victorious staring up into the teacher's worried expression. She had hit me and now looked worried and concerned. "Serves her right," was my thought. It was almost worth the pain, and I wondered if this incident would be my pass for the remainder of a trouble-free year. Surely even Mom could not just brush this off as deserved punishment.

I remained in a leaned back position for several more minutes as the entire class continued to stare down at me. Being the center of all this attention felt a bit heroic. Ms. Heimlich now instructed me to slowly bring my head forward until I sat fully upright. All the eyes were still on me, wondering what was to follow next. "You can now remove the cloth from your nose," she said, staring at my face expectantly.

The bleeding had stopped and as I looked at her face, I could see her lips pressed together with her head slowly shaking in disbelief. She then returned to the front of the class while calling everyone back to attention. Within minutes the bell rang and the class period was over. The teacher, taking me aside, instructed me to go home for the rest of the day and to get myself cleaned up. As I passed my classmates on the way out, I felt that the whole incident had turned into a privilege, as I was allowed to go home. She had tried to punish me but she was now obviously feeling guilty about how this incident had turned out.

It was not until several days later that I learned that Ms. Heimlich had spoken with Mom and apologized for the occurrence. Teachers were usually looked upon as authority figures in the community and were respected for it due to their education. Apologizing to a parent was highly unusual and therefore her apology was a silent victory for me and still brings a smile to my face to this day.

With our young but sensitive minds, we began to realize that several of the teachers reacted to individual students in varying ways. The clearest evidence of this was in the way teachers addressed students by their names. While some were called by their first names, others were called by their last names only. Even their treatment or reaction to student differed. It became obvious that much of this had to do with the economic background of our classmates. Children whose fathers held more prestigious positions seemed to benefit from this. With Dad being held as prisoner of war and Mom receiving only a small monthly government payment, I was usually called by my family name.

This became even more evident in one of my later classes. During a geography class, the girl in front of me was called to the front. Her father had become the director of a local factory. When the teacher had called on her, he smiled and used her first name. He then asked her to show him the city of Hamburg on a large regional map. Embarrassed and not able to do so, she turned to him without speaking. He reached out and gently touched her cheek and in a soft voice said to her, "But Maria," and indicated for her to return to her seat.

Next, while his expression changed to a more serious one, he called out, "Bonisch" in a rather stern voice. It was now my turn to find Hamburg on that large hanging map. Flustered and unable to do so, I raised my shoulders, indicating my inability nonverbally. As I turned toward him, expecting him to command me to sit down as well, his hand hit me across the face and then ordered me to get back to my seat. Although it was not the only incident of this type, it was, however, to become the one that would remain most clearly in my memory. As other students were in similar positions, sharing our feelings and finding the worst description for such teachers helped us to deal with this matter.

On those occasions when we met a teacher in town, we were obligated to remove our hats while bowing to greet him or her in the most respectful manner. Failing to do so would result in being called back to receive a lecture right on the spot. When the situation allowed, we would try to disappear and go into hiding until he or she had passed. Sometimes, while hiding in the alley, the teacher would suddenly appear to confront us and demand to know why we tried to avoid him. Of course we never had a proper excuse and this required an apology and a demonstration of a proper greeting right there and then.

The lack of proper nourishment over the many past war years became an issue, and a school food program was scheduled to be instituted. This was being accomplished with the support of American foreign aid and soon became a reality. It was to assure qualified children one warm meal as part of each school day. Because of our family monthly income, both Gunter and I were able to benefit from this new meal program. As most people suffered from various nutritional deficiencies, this was something Mom was most pleased about.

Although nutritional deficiency was not a concept we children understood, I recall one particular affliction most of us experienced during the cold winter months. With the lack of oil or fat in our diet, the exposed skin on the back of our hands became so dry that it began to crack and bleed, especially around the knuckles. This outbreak was called *Kratze* and is similar to eczema. For lack of medication and out of desperation, people would often apply their own urine on those areas as a method of healing.

To help with the lack of oil, Mom would take us into the nearby forest to collect fallen beechnuts the approximate size of raisins. These were small triangular-shaped seeds that fell off the beech trees annually. With all of us on our knees searching for these small seeds, it took days before we finally filled a bag the approximate size of a potato sack. These seeds could then be exchanged for the equivalent of two liters of cooking oil, something much in demand and needed.

* * *

Help From Our Liberators

Occasionally local American troops served sandwiches for each of the children to enjoy. I recall this so vividly, as we were used to eating mostly the locally made rye bread. American troops, on the other hand, ate white bread instead, something I came to like very quickly. As part of this much-appreciated treat, we usually received a Hershey bar and a stick of chewing gum, items we truly appreciated. To get the most use out of the stick of gum, I would make it last for days on end, and even then it could be shared with a friend. It was through this generosity that we developed a feeling of trust in and reliance upon our liberators, our former enemy.

It was either in late 1946 or early 1947 that we occasionally received powdered milk, butter, and used clothing through the American Catholic Charities. Since Mom was involved in Catholic charity activities, an unpaid church activity, she would usually coordinate the distribution of these items, and this placed us on the receiving end as well. Gunter and I usually delivered the rationed items to the various local Catholic families, who truly appreciated even a stick of butter. One such supply consisted of peanut butter, a product most German people had never heard of or tasted before, and it became an item of much debate.

During one such distribution, I became the lucky recipient of a pair of used corduroy trousers. They were of a light brown color and fit me quite well. I had wanted to save them only for school, but at the same time Mom was concerned that I might outgrow them soon and would have to pass them on to my younger brother, Wolfgang. Some

American boy had worn these before, and I wondered if he could ever know how much I appreciated having them.

Our friends next door had an aunt in the United States and were now receiving an occasional package from there. I recall admiring a new belt that each of the boys had received and couldn't help but wonder what America was really like. The thought of going there someday seemed like reaching for the stars. Although it seemed impossible, it was nonetheless exciting to think about. Travel—even a short train ride into the next town—became an exciting event for me. I soon realized that I had a travel fever that was far less evident in my brothers or sister.

On those occasions when I mentioned to Mom my early desire to go to America some day, she would usually start to talk about Dad coming home soon and that I needed to be there. I was only eight and realized that it would be many years before I could even begin to think about such a venture. For now, the hope of Dad's homecoming was foremost in all our minds.

* * *

New Bells for Our Church Tower

It was ironic to think that our brass church bells had possibly been turned into bullets. The war had required many such sacrifices and had left our church tower with only a small bell for several years now. Although it was a Protestant church, it was such an important icon that we all felt a certain closeness to it. There the town's occupants were baptized, confirmed, married, and finally buried. Its steeple was always a welcoming and familiar sight when returning home from outside of town.

Now we were to receive two new bells not made of brass, but of cast iron material. The day of their arrival was declared a holiday and so children and adults were lining the sidewalk to welcome these long-awaited items. There was something very revered about their arrival as the flatbed truck slowly drove through town and toward the church. Due to their size and weight, a special scaffold had been erected to hoist them to the upper level of the tower. Within just a few days' time, the bells were in place and could now be rung. First there was the ringing of just one bell, which could easily be determined by its singular ding-dong sound. Then the second bell chimed in, and soon they gave off their sounds to the community.

For us they became more than just bells calling us for church service on Sunday morning. They would ring out the hour of day, while also indicating the fifteen-minute increments of each hour. If a person had died during the night, the bells would ring the following morning, informing the community that one of its members had passed on. During harvest time, the bells were rung in three successions each morning to give credence to this important period. Also, they would indicate when a wedding or funeral took place, and the citizens quickly learned their intended messages and began to rely on them for the daily events.

Herr Schaper, an old gentlemen and original citizen of Duingen, had the responsibility to assure that the bells would ring at the required times each day. I had asked him one day if I could watch him while he rang the bells, and he just nodded his head. After this first experience, I made it a point to accompany him more often. He was a very patient man who truly lived by his pocket watch but never exhibited any hurry. He spoke very little but seemed to tolerate my hanging around.

I just appeared at the back of church by the old tower door whenever I wanted to join him. I knew that he would never be late and I would first hear the creaking iron gate leading into the graveyard behind the church. Seconds later, he appeared at the back door, about two minutes before the bells needed to be rung. This gave us sufficient time to climb the old, worn-out wooden staircase to the first level. Without ever speaking, he would indicate to me when to press the start button. I then quickly ran to the next level to watch the two massive bells swing into action until the inner pendulum made contact with the bell housing and soon they were in full swing, chiming away.

It was easy for me to imagine being inside a castle while climbing the old, worn-out wooden stairs of the thousand-year-old tower. Even during the daytime there was a spookiness about the place, and I would frequently assure myself that Mr. Schaper was still nearby. He seemed so at peace while doing his duty and somehow I couldn't help but feel how much he actually fit the surroundings of this old and historic place. Occasionally a coffin with a body would be stored at the bottom of the tower while awaiting the funeral, but he hardly ever took notice of it.

From the second floor inside the tower, a low, worn-out wooden door lead to the organ loft and into the attached sixteenth-century church. The old wooden balconies and the straight green painted pews reflected a stricter Reformation era. It was quite exciting to explore the pathways with their low ceilings between the tower and the church. I quickly came to realize that, although I enjoyed doing this by day, I would not want to be there at night.

From up there, one could overlook the entire graveyard behind the church with its many old headstones. The combination of the gray stone tower, the church, and the graveyard could easily stir our young minds into a world of ghosts and bodies rising from their graves.

* * *

Our Games of Dare

Occasionally during the late summer evenings, we would walk behind the church and face the graveyard, with the church wall as safety behind us. On our previous visits we had noticed that some of the older and larger graves were covered with two large stone plates. Over time the mortar between the plates had eroded and left a small gap down the middle, where the aged stones met. By dropping little pebbles between them, we could hear that they landed on what seemed to be a metal box inside the several-hundred-year-old vault. Often this became a test of bravery to do this by oneself while the rest of the boys watched from a safe distance.

On summer evenings, shortly after supper, we would all meet again by our usual place at the corner of Hauptstrasse and Zweftje in front of the shoe repair shop. By now, the little shoe shop had closed, but the faint odor of leather and glue still permeated the air. This was the time for playing hide-and-go-seek or robber-and-bandits, whereby half the group had to chase the other half through town. We, as the youngest, usually became the chasing team. Occasionally we would ring someone's doorbell and then run away. If nothing could be decided upon, competing to shoot sparrows with our slingshots often became the activity of the evening.

One evening, while meeting at our usual spot and trying to decide what to do next, we noticed our police officer, Herr Wachtmeister Busch, walking toward us but still at a great distance. He was sort of a proud-looking man, usually with his hands folded behind his back as he walked very erect and at an even pace. His face was always serious and his voice was unusually low and authoritative. We feared him, as he usually confiscated several of our sleds during the winter months for sledding on official highways. He would usually just appear in spite of our caution and looking out for him.

He was now coming closer and so we quickly moved across Zweftje to hide behind the corner of the adjacent barn just opposite the shoe repair shop. From here we could watch him without being seen. By now he was less than a hundred feet away from us, and although we had nothing to fear, hiding like this seemed somehow exciting. Suddenly and without warning, one of the older boys shouted out his name, "Busch, Busch," intended in a sort of an insulting manner. Immediately, we all began to run up Zweftje and away from him. This was totally unexpected, as it had not been previously talked about. We knew that he was much too proud to run after us and so once we reached a safe distance, we stopped. What if he saw us? Where would we go and hide? We looked nervously around us. "The graveyard," someone said, and instantly we all began running in that direction.

He had surprised us before and it was possible that he could suddenly appear at any place. We waited until dark before we decided whether to leave our hiding spot. It now became an issue whether to be here at this spooky place at night or face being caught while sneaking home. Coming home too late after dark would give us problems with our mothers as well. We finally decided to leave in groups of two, as this seemed the least obvious if caught. The next day we learned that everyone had made it home without any problems. It was understood that we still had to be cautious for several more days and avoid contact with our local police officer. We resolved this by simply meeting at a different location for the next few days.

* * *

Besides spending many afternoons on the nearby farm, we often played in the woods to the east of town. Since we had to walk about a third of a mile uphill to reach the edge of the woods, this part of the forest was known by the locals as the mount. There was also a large forest to the west of town, which we simply referred to as the forest. From the top of the mount we could overlook the entire village, including the neighboring town to the north called Weenzen. Straight across town to the west, well behind the forest, were gently sloping hills called Ith and Hills. It was a very peaceful and familiar sight from up here on the mount. This was also where we felt totally free to roam and play. Here we explored the traces of wild boars or searched for fox holes. We could build huts out of branches and pretend to be Indians or often simply sit up high in our favorite trees. Up here we could be heroes or bandits or just ourselves with only our imagination to guide us. Here we created our own world until the church bells called us home for supper.

Military convoys were still frequently coming through town, something I always took notice of. I often waved to the soldiers on the back of their passing trucks and felt special when several of them returned my greeting with a smile. There was something about their brown uniforms with their net-covered helmets that I admired and enjoyed seeing. Other than the military vehicles and the farmers' horse-drawn wagons, there was still little traffic that passed through town. As most convoys were led by jeeps, it soon became a vehicle that I greatly admired in my young mind. I frequently fantasized about owning such a vehicle someday and pictured myself driving it on the many dirt roads in our area.

As we were now entering the fall season, it was again time for all to help get the potatoes out of the ground. Mom again would work the hardest by digging them up with a pitchfork, while all four of us children would then collect them after her and place them inside a hundred-pound potato sack. It was also our job to make certain that none of the potatoes were left in the ground.

Our favorite time was the mid-afternoon break, when we ate our syrup sandwiches Mom had brought with her. It was jokingly named a poor man's meal. It consisted of a slice of rye bread covered with a sweet syrup that we annually extracted from locally grown sweet beats. Sausage or other sandwich spread was still being sold under ration stamps, and so this simple substitute became quite popular not only locally but throughout Germany.

By late afternoon we began our way home, with Gunter and I pulling our loaded hand wagon back to town. Marlene was still only four, so she was allowed to ride on top of the potato sacks while Mom pushed from behind and could easily keep an eye on her. Once home, the harvest was carried into our small but cool potato cellar for storage.

We were still gleaning the fields after the farmers had brought in their crops. It had become a standard practice for many families and helped subsidize our food needs. During the course of an afternoon, we could sometimes dig up leftover potatoes to fill a half sack. Missed wheat husks were collected one by one, and the kernels were later turned in for a small bag of flour. Often there were several families on the same field, so it became a rush to get to the ungleaned areas first.

Late in the season was the time for leftover sweet beets. As soon as a farmer had finished harvesting his field, we would (with his permission of course) go over it to look for beets that had been missed and were still buried in the ground. Due to their large size, they became more difficult to dig up. Once we had collected a sufficient amount, they were washed and boiled in a large kettle. Through this process they turned into a dark and sweet syrup that served us as sandwich spread throughout the year. Cooling this syrup on a stick or spoon would also serve as a substitute for suckers or candy, and so it was well liked. For us children this annual event of making syrup was a special day we always looked forward to. It was also the one day when we could eat our fill of this wonderful sweet substance.

By year end it became clear that we would soon undergo a change in currency from the current reichsmark to the new deutsche mark. This change would also bring about the elimination of the long-used ration cards. It was not totally clear how this change might influence our future lives, but the adults seemed to welcome this expected reform.

I was now eight-and-a-half and well into my second year at school, and I had moved on with my classmates. Not passing a grade was of course a concern for most of us. It not only required us to take the same year over again, but more so it became a social stigma that we dreaded most of all. Occasionally as part of our early geography, we were shown movies of faraway countries and cultures. These were by far my favorite class periods, and it was then I realized that travel would have to be part of my future life.

Through the engagement of a cousin, we had come to know the family of her future spouse. Her soon-to-be father-in-law had once owned a farm somewhere in one of the German-African colonies.

During the war years these colonies were lost and so he returned to Germany. He was now well up in years, although his children's ages ranged close to ours. I recall admiring his many pictures of his life in Africa. More so, I was fascinated by every story he was so willing to tell us. For him these were obviously proud years as part of a vanishing ruling class on the African continent.

* * *

By Christmas 1947, Dad was still held as prisoner in Yugoslavia. German soldiers who had been taken captive by American or British troops were being released and began arriving home. Those who became captives in Russia remained prisoners, and it was not known if and when these men would be allowed to return home. Siberia became known as the worst area of the Russian prison camps and horrible stories began circulate.

The search for lost relatives and those missing in action continued to remain strong. German soldiers usually referred to fellow soldiers as Kameraden (comrades), a term I always found caring and touching. While listening to the sad songs of lonely soldiers, dreaming of being home or of their comrades who had been killed, we envisioned our fathers so far away and did not know their situations. The words of these songs had a very special impact on us.

Mom had been able to purchase our ration of brown coal. Our Catholic friend, employed as forest worker, again shared his extra entitlement of wood with us. Gunter and I would saw the meter lengths into short pieces and then split them for use in our kitchen and living room stoves. None of the other rooms had stoves and so could not be heated. Once Gunter took a break, Wolfgang and I had the responsibility to stack the split pieces along the house wall.

We were again in the middle of winter, and to conserve firewood and coal, Mom would usually only keep the kitchen stove lit, so this small room became the center of most family activity. There was hardly ever a time for Mom to really relax. Refrigerators or washing machines were not yet in use, so the washboard was the most commonly used instrument for doing laundry. I recall her often bent over the washboard while pearls of sweat ran down her face, as she would frequently try to keep the dark strands of hair out of her face. It would take her a good part of the day to complete the wash, until all pieces of clothing were hung out on the clotheslines for drying. During the winter months, the clothing would often swing on the line, completely frozen stiff.

As a means of preserving food for the following year, vegetables and fruits had to be prepared and canned into glass jars. In the evening after supper, Mom would again wash the dishes in her tiny single sink, which only had a cold-water faucet to assist her. All necessary hot water had to be heated on the kitchen stove. This was a time when we did our homework while Mom now sat and mended the holes in our socks or even knitted new ones. Her hands were always busy doing something. Grandma was also part of our household and had all her meals with us. Usually after supper she would retreat to her own room for the evening. Because of the tight living conditions, Gunter and I had to sleep together in Grandma's room. Although she had her bed at the other end of the narrow room, once it was lights out, she would often tell us about her younger days and those of Dad. This was something we always enjoyed but more importantly, it helped me to relax.

The Fire Next Door

Grandma's room had two windows, one facing south and the other facing east. Our bed was located along the window to the south, and so often in the evening or morning we could talk to our friends just a few feet across the yard at the neighboring house. This became an almost daily routine, especially during the warm summer evenings when we could talk directly from our open windows.

The window to the east faced a carpenter shop also just located across our backyard. Both Grandma's room and the wood shop were located on the second floor, and the windows faced each other directly, with only about ten feet between them. It was on one of those winter evenings, as we were just getting ready for bed, when we noticed bright flames inside the work shop. The instant shouting of "Fire!" echoed through the house and across the yard, and people appeared and began to form a bucket line in the dark in an effort to extinguish the flames. Gunter ran out to help while Grandma and I watched the flames becoming stronger. While seeing the flames from the window, I became shaken with fear, as I associated this event with flashbacks of the war. There was a lot of shouting and running outside, and we could see water being thrown into the room. It seemed almost hopeless from our position, but soon the large flames began to diminish until they were finally brought under control. Soon only smoke filled the room and people were still talking busily outside.

As I began to relax, I wondered how it was possible to get people to respond so quickly and how they were able to coordinate this firefighting effort so successfully. The place being a woodworking shop created some concern that the fire could possibly start up again. Once all the smoke had cleared, the room was carefully checked to assure that it was in fact safe. It was quite late that night before we were finally able to return to bed and to sleep. The following day we learned that Gunter and his friend from next door, whose father owned the shop, had tried to build something from scrap wood. When leaving the shop, apparently neither of them had bothered to make sure that no fire was left in the stove. As a result, a spark had ignited nearby wood chips and quickly spread from there. With the exception of a good lecture, no punishment was given to either.

* * *

From Reichsmark to Deutsche Mark

Early during 1948, there was much talk about the changeover to a new German currency and the elimination of ration stamps. I had turned nine at the end of April and had now started my third school year. June 21, 1948, less than two months later, was the date set for the currency changeover from the reichsmark to the deutsche mark, which was also called DM for short. Those fortunate enough to have savings of the old reichsmark could now exchange them by receiving DM 6.50 for each 100 reichsmark. June 21, 1948 became a day well remembered, as items that were in short supply under the old ration system were suddenly available overnight. Store windows that were previously empty were suddenly filled with goods. It was quite an adjustment to suddenly be able to purchase anything one needed by simply just paying with the new currency.

Most amazing for us children was that we could now buy candy or chocolate at the grocery store, provided we had the money. With Dad still being held as prisoner of war, Mom now received forty deutsche mark per family member each month from the government. Since this was barely enough to provide for a family of five, we needed to continue to grow much of our own food. Although everything seemed to be now available in abundance, we continued to live on a tight budget, as did most people in those days.

It was a new experience to be able to walk into any bakery and purchase two loaves of bread without any questions being asked. The bakery just around the corner began to sell ice-cream cones, and soon they opened their backyard as an ice-cream shop. With this change came a new energy and freedom that was most encouraging. Before long, there were occasional movies shown in one of the larger restaurant halls. The first experience of seeing people moving on a large screen was fascinating for us. Grandma also received a small pension and became our source of borrowing occasional movie money, which she was never repaid.

June 23, 1948, only two days after this important date in West German history, the Soviets posted a blockade around the Russian sector of Berlin and the East German part occupied by them. Although this news meant little to us children then, it seemed that most people had relatives in those areas, and so it became a much talked about issue. As more news was received over the next few months, we felt fortunate to be able to move about so freely.

* * *

A Dangerous Rafting Experience

It was now summer and we were in the middle of our school vacation. The old town swimming pool, located about a half mile outside of town, was still closed, but the pool remained full of water. Someone in our group had noticed a raft made up of a few short logs tied tightly together with ropes. It was at the deep end of the pool. This information created an immediate curiosity in all of us and we needed to see it. We entered the pool area, which was all uncut grass, through a narrow opening at the back hedges, and we were directly at the deepest part of the pool. The raft was floating in the middle of the old pool and so it was impossible for us to reach it from the edge. Gunter and Helmut, who were the oldest among us, found a tree branch long enough to hook onto the raft and to pull it toward us.

While Gunter held onto the raft to prevent it from drifting away, Helmut decided to try to stand on it while holding onto the edge of the pool. It seemed to support him without showing any sign of sinking. Feeling more confident, he began to sit down on it. Now holding onto the branch, he allowed the raft to drift slowly toward the middle while Gunter followed him, holding firm at the other end of the branch. "Get me a paddle," said Helmut, now very confident and smiling, and someone handed him a piece of a branch. "Who wants to come on with me?" Helmut now asked, quite proud of himself. Gunter was the first to volunteer, and so Helmut paddled the raft close to the ladder to make it easier for Gunter to climb on and keep the raft steady. Soon both were sliding to the middle of the pool while smiling and enjoying themselves.

"Can I be next?" I asked, hesitating somewhat but excited. The raft again pulled up to the ladder, as this seemed to be the easiest way to get on and off. Gunter got off and Helmut now seemed to have taken on the role of captain. While carefully climbing on, I realized that I couldn't swim, but then, none of us could, so why should I hesitate? We now began to leave the edge while Helmut was using his makeshift paddle to steer the raft toward the middle of the pool like he had before. It was fun and everybody except Jurgen now wanted their turn. During all these rides, Helmut remained on the raft, now very confident in handling the maneuvering.

Everybody had now taken their turn, some even twice, with the exception of Jurgen, who didn't want to get on the raft. He was now being urged to take his turn, as he was guaranteed to like it. Finally after some urging, Jurgen reluctantly agreed to get on, with Helmut still in control. This would be our last ride, as we planned to return home afterward.

Jurgen seated himself next to Helmut, and they pushed off from the edge, slowly drifting toward the center. Now at least all of us had a turn at this fun. Helmut was slowly paddling to cause the raft to go into a slow turn, something he had done previously and it had given the riders a special thrill. They began their drift back toward the ladder when suddenly the rope holding the logs together gave out and the logs quickly came apart. As both Helmut and Jurgen fell into the water, the logs floated off in different directions, leaving them no support. Helmut was closer to the edge of the pool and was able to grab onto someone's outstretched hand. Jurgen was farther away and out of reach, and was now wildly struggling. He quickly disappeared from the surface. Within seconds he reappeared, still wildly struggling while gasping for air. Again he disappeared under the surface but soon reappeared with a frightened look and his arms swinging wildly around in desperation. Once more he disappeared underwater, struggling for air.

During all this he had come a little closer to the ladder but not close enough to grab hold. Gunter now quickly climbed down the ladder into the water and, while holding on with one hand, reached out as far as possible with the other. As Jurgen surfaced again, Gunter quickly grabbed his struggling arm and pulled him toward the ladder. Jurgen now frantically grabbed for it while Gunter made sure not to lose him. While holding onto the ladder, Jurgen was still gasping for air. We all now ran over to help pull him up onto the grass. It took a while until he regained his breath. The rest of us hovered around him. All of this had happened so quickly and unexpectedly that we were all stunned. By saving Jurgen's life, Gunter now became somewhat of a hero for us. We waited some time before we finally decided to return to town.

Although we had decided to keep the matter quiet, the news of this event got out rather quickly. It was just too important for us to keep from other friends until it reached our families. I don't recall receiving any punishment for our risky venture. The fact that Gunter had rescued Jurgen probably aided in this. We never again attempted to ride the raft; nor did we know of anyone else who attempted to do so after our mishap. We often talked about this event, which remained with us as one of those daring childhood occurrences.

* * *

Summer 1948

It was now mid-summer and we were enjoying our annual six-week vacation from school. Without the burden of school during the long, warm summer days, life could hardly be any better. Just outside of town, well-plotted fields of wheat, oats, and rye bordered the main roads. Their color was beginning to change from their original green to their final golden yellow. It was a sign that they had now reached their nearly full height. We had become quite proficient at identifying the type of crop between the similar-looking wheat and rye by simply gauging their height and by the shape of their husks. On a windy day, the top-heavy blades would sway in unison, giving the appearance of waves during a rough sea. I knew even then that I had no interest of ever becoming a farmer, and yet I admired their ability to grow something so perfect.

Loitering on the nearby farm was still something we did on a regular basis. The odor from the large manure pile in the center of the farmyard and that from the cows and pigs was ever-present. Although it was unpleasant, it did not deter us from wanting to be there. Contrary to this unpleasant odor, I enjoyed the ammonia-like smell of the horse stable that could occasionally pierce one's nostrils. The fact that they were such clean animals probably made the difference for me. Even when work horses left their droppings on the road while moving through town, someone would usually recover them for their garden.

With late summer came harvest time, when farmers raced against the weather to bring their crops into the barns. This was their busiest time of the year and so we could often make ourselves useful. Handling a team of horses and wagon was truly my favorite farm activity. Being in control over these large animals gave me a sense of pride, and it never failed to amaze me how they obeyed every one of my commands. While one of us boys handled the team, it freed up an additional farmhand to help load the wagons in the field.

As the bales were being lifted up onto the wagon, the dogs would chase the field mice that usually hid beneath those stacked bales and now tried to scatter in all directions.

Once the load was delivered to the barn, the real work began, as the bales of straw now had to be fed through the thresher to extract the grain and then were stacked for storage. All of this was not without danger, not to mention the extreme heat and dust inside the barn. Although these were days of hard work, we usually found enjoyment in being a part of this busy time. It also gave us an appreciation for farm life, where work began before sunrise and ended late in the evening. Besides the plowing, planting, and harvesting, the farm animals needed to be taken care of, regardless of whether it was a weekday or a Sunday. Most of all, it was the smell of the farm life that we associated with farmers, even at their Sunday best. I often wondered why anyone would choose this lifestyle, and yet I had a certain admiration for the dedication to their work that benefited all of us.

For us boys, much of this activity was enjoyable, as it offered us the opportunity to ride a horse or to ride along on a tractor or even to milk a cow. Without realizing it then, we also learned some basic lessons of hard work and responsibility that would remain with us.

A Few Messy Events

I was now proudly going on ten but still one of the youngest in our group of friends. During the summer months and until about mid fall, the farmer's cows needed to be led outside of town to one of the several pastures for grazing. This was a task often given to us boys. The herd could range between sixteen and twenty animals. We had become quite proficient in leading them in a single file to allow the occasional traffic to pass without hindrance. Most of the pastures were located about a mile distant. While walking behind the cows, one had to be careful of the ever-swinging tail and the occasional surprise coming from beneath it. We usually enjoyed this task, as it made us feel important to know that the farmer trusted us with his animals. The fact that we had control over them gave us youngsters a powerful feeling.

On one such occasion, the foreman had asked us to take Ella, a tall, aging farm horse, along for the grazing. She had been part of the farm for as long as any of us could remember. We shared a certain fondness for her, as we had ridden her and worked with her and knew her to be a very gentle and trusting animal. I was entrusted to lead her, and so she became my only concern as I followed the cows and the boys controlling them down the main road through town. The herd was now stretched out, as they were being kept to the side of the road. With this many cows, it was quite common and amusing to leave a fresh trail of cow droppings along the way. We knew to keep a safe distance for exactly those unpredictable reasons.

Once we arrived at the open pasture, we knew that the cows would eat constantly, only stopping to look up occasionally while chewing the fresh grass. Their udders became larger as the afternoon progressed, and milking would be done after they returned home. While they were grazing, we could play our games nearby or simply lie in the grass. A narrow creek wound its way through the pasture and so we often tried to catch fish with our bare hands, but usually without much success. One of the few deeper and wider spots served us well for bathing, especially on those hot days.

Ella, the horse, had eaten some of the grass and, totally trusting her, we had left her to wander about selecting her own spots to graze. After grazing a while, she began to lie down completely on her side with her head resting in the grass. At first it seemed very natural for her to want to rest; however, the way she was lying began to arouse our attention.

I walked over to her and began stroking her long brown neck. She didn't move but opened her eyes, which seemed to show a gentle tiredness. By now several of the other boys had come over to gaze at the horse's body below. We began to wonder whether something was wrong with her, and so we tried to get her on her feet. The normally obedient animal would not even lift her head.

By now all the boys had gathered around trying to guess what might possibly be ailing her. We had often watched the veterinarian treat animals and we were soon in agreement that Ella must be suffering from bloating caused by eating the green grass. The cows continued to eat undisturbed, and so we could concentrate all our efforts on the horse. From her gentle nature, we all really liked and trusted her and so promptly decided that we needed to help her by applying the method we had observed used by the vet.

Helmut was the first to kneel behind the resting animal. While indicating for one of us to lift her tail away from the body, he carefully began to push his right hand into the animal's rectum. Ella made no efforts to resist as one of the other boys continued to stroke her neck while softly talking to her. By now Helmut began to retract his arm and immediately displayed a hand full of warm manure from inside the animal. He then repeated the procedure, going just a little deeper

71

each time. Still there was no resistance from her. We realized that a kick with her hind legs could severely injure anyone struck by it.

While watching Helmut, most of us were now getting anxious to try our hand at this. Being one of the younger kids in the group, I had to wait my turn. As I finally knelt behind the horse, I nervously began to push my fist through the opening and slowly continued to slide down while moving my fist from side to side to help the move. I was now nearly up to my elbow and could feel the warmth of her body. My hand was smaller than some of the others, which also made the slide somewhat easier. While extending my fingers, I began to feel an obstruction and so began to draw some of it into my hand. Exclaiming to have made contact, I began to withdraw my arm until I could proudly display the results. I was then encouraged to repeat this procedure once more, again with success. Soon everybody had their turn and it was time to await the results of our effort.

During all this excitement we had nearly forgotten about the cows, but from experience we knew that they would not wander off. Most of us were now padding or stroking some part of the horse, hoping to help her by doing so. We then waited to see if our service had helped her, as we felt certain that it should reduce any internal pressure.

It wasn't too long before she began to lift her head and our hopes began to rise. "Let's try to get her on her feet," someone said, and while we pulled on her harness, she began to get up. Since I had taken charge of her at the beginning, I was now proudly walking her without any obvious signs of difficulty. We felt quite proud of having been able to help her in this manner and through it we felt an even greater closeness to this gentle aging animal.

At about half past five, we began to round up the herd to lead them back to the main road and home. The animals knew the routine and obediently started to turn on to the road leading back to town. It was now more difficult for the cows to walk, as their udders were now bulging from being filled with milk. The first part of the road went uphill before it leveled off just prior to entering the town. I was again at the rear leading Ella and could oversee the entire herd as it quickly stretched out along the road. This was usually the time when someone would occasionally grab onto a cow's tail to be pulled along. The frightened animals would then usually try to run with the bulging udders getting in the way, and so the boy would then let go of the tail to allow the animal to calm down.

I could see Helmut just grabbing the tail of the cow in front of him. Just as the animal started its forward lurch, Helmut was yanked along, almost losing his balance. He still held onto the tail and it was now extended straight out. Suddenly, a stream of green cow poop shot out of the animal's rear at such force that it covered the unsuspecting Helmut from his head to his feet. He immediately let go of the tail and came to a halt as the green, stinky poop was dripping from his entire front body. Holding out his arm to the side, he began staring down his front in total disbelief.

The cow had run a short distance and then slowed to a normal walk. By now some of the boys had realized Helmut's misfortune and were laughing wildly while pointing at him as he stood motionless in disbelief, still looking at himself in disgust. Most had had similar close call experiences in the past but were usually able to avoid this unexpected reaction from the cows they followed.

By now I had caught up with him. "What am I going to do?" was his first concern. "I can't go through town looking like this," he went on, still looking at himself. The others had realized their responsibility for the safety of the herd and so quickly ran after them to guide them through town and home. Helmut had now walked to the side of the road. He began pulling bunches of the tall grass to clean himself as best as could be done. The shallow ditch to the side of the road held little water. With the help of some grass and the water, he was able to remove most of the unpleasant substance from his face, shirt, shorts, arms, and legs. Although he looked somewhat better, he could not totally escape the smell associated with the mishap. "How do I look?" he asked, looking at me, awaiting my response. "It's not bad. Let's get going. You can wash up when we get back" was the best I could say, trying not to laugh while holding onto Ella.

When we finally approached the entrance to the farm, the group and a few additional boys were waiting for Helmut to once again laugh about his misfortune. The event was then being retold, with each of the boys presenting his own version. It was the gross nature of this occurrence that made it so lively for us to rehash again and again in the most colorful manner. Even Helmut gave us his version of the experience in a most descriptive way, and I could see how everyone around simply enjoyed talking and laughing about this without seeming to tire of it.

Once we had finally exhausted this colorful topic sufficiently, the conversation turned to Ella and how we had worked on her back at the pasture. It was something we all felt proud about, and we were eager to share this with the other boys who had not been with us. These, like many other events, remained with us and often became the subject of conversation, which always resulted in many good laughs.

* * *

The Old Blacksmith Shop

Somewhat diagonal from our house across Hauptstrasse was a short back street that again connected the Hauptstrasset with the Triftstrasse. From here, just around the corner, was one of the two blacksmith shops in town. On a quiet day, we could hear the faint hammering of hot metal being formed into the desired shape. The hammering was always followed by the higher pitch bouncing of the hammer on the anvil until it settled to a stop. The gray stone walls inside of his shop were covered with a dark soot. The blacksmith's tools were located on worn-out shelves and hanging from the dark walls. It was in part this type of atmosphere that so attracted me to his shop.

The blacksmith himself was an older man, by my young estimation. He was known as a master blacksmith, and his work truly reflected his skill and dedication to his profession. He occasionally interrupted his work to quickly wipe the sweat from his forehead with the use of his lower arm or the back of his hand. With the help of long metal tongs, he would move his work piece from the fire to the anvil. Here he immediately began hammering the red-hot iron piece while occasionally breaking to let the hammer bounce off the anvil several times before continuing the shaping. It was a little like musical rhythms, as the tone and frequency changed with the constant alternating from hammering to the bouncing of the anvil and back at the iron. It was interesting to watch him skillfully shape the metal pieces into the many different forms. Once the metal had lost its red-hot glow, he would swing back to the hearth. While working the piece into the fire, his other hand worked the bellows to fan the flames. It was a ritual that I often watched from the entrance of his shop, and it mesmerized me.

Much of his time was taken up shoeing the many farm horses in town. This seemed especially hard work, as he would have to lift each of the heavy legs of the horse several times while fitting the metal shoe. Again he would move from the horse to the hearth and then to the anvil to hammer it into the desired shape. While the piece was still hot, he would fit it to the horse's hoof, which resulted in a burning smell and smoke. Although the burning smell was rather strong, I did not find it unpleasant. Once he had reached the desired fit, he nailed the shoe to the bottom of the horse's hoof. The nails, because of their length, came out of the side of the hoof and were cut off and filed down. He never seemed to fear the horse's reaction as he performed his hard work.

Watching this blacksmith was not only interesting for me then; it was almost soothing. He never seemed to make a big to-do about the planning and the laying out of his work; nor did he ever say much. I often came to his shop just to observe him in his work. For me, it was as if time stood still there, as his shop differed very little from the old story books of so long ago.

The Terrible Thunderstorm

As boys, we could usually make something interesting out of most situations. We would find something to entertain us when the sun was shining or we played inside the farmer's barn or hayloft when it rained. Often after a heavy rain shower, we enjoyed building dams at the curb along our main road just to see how far we could back up the water. This activity often became a competition to see who among us would be the most successful. To get a head start, we would often begin this process while a heavy thunderstorm was just beginning to let up, and we didn't mind being soaked by the warm rain. We were more concerned about gathering enough mud to make each event even bigger than the previous one. Obviously, being so engaged in our activity, we took little notice of the distant lightning and thunder. This, however, was soon to change.

It was a late summer afternoon, and farmers were rushing to bring in as much of their crop as possible just ahead of the approaching dark clouds. By about five o'clock we could hear the beginnings of the distant thunder, and so my brothers and I began to talk about the potential for building our dams following the rain. The thunder was quickly becoming louder, an indication for us that the thunderstorm was heading in our direction. Soon we noticed the occasional lightning and from the time between the lightning and the responding thunder, we had learned to count and determine the approximate distance of the storm. It had become a sort of a game for us, as if we had uncovered something of magic.

The intervals between the lightning and the thunder were quickly becoming shorter, until the response was almost immediate. It began to rain, and the frequency of the lightning was now in rapid succession, followed each time by the exploding sound of the thunder. The lightning, rather than being in the form of the usual downward flash, looked like exploding fireballs followed by an instant crash of thunder until both lightning and thunder almost seemed to be a continuing event. We could no longer distinguish between the unprecedented explosions of the fireball lightning and the enormous instant crashes of the thunder. With this it had turned a darkness that only intensified the constant flashing explosions. It was the first time that I feared the effects of any thunderstorm I had ever experienced. In a way it reminded me of the anxious waiting we used to endure in our potato cellar during the many air raids of previous years.

We all huddled in our small kitchen, and because of the darkness Mom had turned on the single ceiling light. She had just sat down between the kitchen table and the sink when suddenly a lightning ball explosion seemed to occur right inside our kitchen. The severity of the explosion, with its indescribable bright flash, had us all in shock. Fire was shooting out of the electrical outlet, burning the side of the nearby kitchen cabinet. The light bulb from our ceiling light exploded and the glass pieces from it landed on Mom's head, and it all happened in a matter of just a second.

It took several more seconds before we were able to move or even speak. Mom was still holding her hands above her head as if expecting more debris to come down on her. There was a burning smell combined with smoke, and the side of the kitchen cabinet was blackened by the flames from the nearby outlet. We had momentarily forgotten about the raging thunderstorm that continued outside.

"We have been hit by lightning" was my first response, and without a further thought I ran out of the kitchen door and upstairs toward the attic to see if the roof was on fire. Gunter had followed me and we reached the attic stairs together. It took both of us to push the attic door open as we expectantly began to smell for smoke while hurriedly looked for a possible fire. Convinced that everything looked okay, we ran back down to the kitchen to report our findings. Mom, together with Grandma, Wolfgang, and Marlene, were wildly discussing what had just happened. We all agreed that the unusual ball type lightning explosion had just occurred right here in the kitchen among us without causing us personal harm. The only victim had been Mom when the light bulb exploded above her head. She was still picking pieces of the thin glass from her dark hair.

The storm was letting up now, as the time between lightning and thunder became longer and the sounds began to fade in the distance. The rain continued to fall for a while and for a change I was not so anxious to go outside to build my dam. As the rain finally stopped, voices could be heard coming from outside as people began to gather to discuss the unusual phenomenon we had all just experienced. We quickly learned that the same unusual lightning had struck several houses in the neighborhood. The owner of a nearby barber shop described how the flames had shot out of his electric haircutting devices when lightning struck his shop, scaring both him and his seated customer to no avail.

The incident remained with me and for years to come I was frightened just to learn of any expected thunderstorms. Several weeks later, on our way home from our garden, we had to take shelter with people along the way while a similar storm came through the area. Out of fear and in final desperation I had to ask Mom if we could pray, and we did so briefly and quietly. Other than on this occasion, I never expressed this fear to Mom or anyone else and eventually overcame most of it.

Return to School with a New View of Girls

By mid August, at age nine and a half, it was time to return to school, as our summer vacation had ended. I was now in my third year and began to really dislike school. Perhaps it was our teacher, who was old by our estimation and definitely of the old school. He too would not hesitate to hit his students but often preferred to squeeze one's upper arm and watch the one being punished squirm in pain. While performing this painful punishment, he angrily talked to his victim, and fine spit would be flying from his mouth. The class would sit in silence while watching the angry event being played out in front of them.

My favorite time became the break between classes, when we could get outside the school building and into the yard. None of the classrooms had clocks and so I recall anxiously waiting for the bell to ring. I had also learned from the behavior of the teachers when the class period came to an end. Some would wash their hands to get rid of the chalk just minutes before class ended. Others just walked to their desk and began to sit down while giving final instructions to the class. This was usually the time I began to relax and looked forward to getting out. Since the beginning of our new school year, I had begun to notice Ursula, who now sat one row over and to my right. She seemed friendly and usually smiled when I happened to look at her. Once outside, I encouraged my friend Rudie that we should join the group of girls that Ursula was part of, even if that meant joining them in their silly games. In doing so, I usually managed to hold her hand while playing their games, something that gave me a good yet unfamiliar feeling. Soon the bell would call us back for our next class and in my mind I would already plan for the next break.

When not being with the other boys, Rudie and I began to enjoy playing with the local girls. There was Analiese and Suzanne, who lived just around the corner and who were usually eager to play hopscotch or other games with us. Another girl was Siegried, the sister of one of the guys in our group, who lived just up the street. She was by far one of the prettiest girls who now began to hang around more with us. Although she was pretty by our estimation, she was also quite bossy, something that easily intimidated us. Then there was Monica, who lived near the market square. Since we would occasionally play with one or both of her brothers, we came to know her as their sister. She too was quite attractive but was quite controlling. With this personality she would argue with any of us and would not hesitate to physically fight, as this was often a means of settling an argument or disagreement. Ursula lived farther away and was not part of our normal neighborhood group, and so I looked forward to seeing her at school each day.

It was traditional for girls to wear dresses or skirts and they usually had their hair braided into pigtails. Pulling on their pigtails was usually a way of getting their attention, although it was not always appreciated by them. Rudie and I became most comfortable with Analiese and Suzanne from around the corner. They would usually agree with anything we suggested, which made our playing together quite enjoyable.

Hopscotch became one of our favorite games. It required only something to mark out the game on the ground and a stone to indicate the square to be avoided while jumping. It gave us boys the occasional glimpse of the girls' underpants while they were jumping, and we found this to be a start of a new curiosity.

* * *

Our First Circus

By mid August, posters were being circulated of a circus coming to town for a three-day performance. Several days later, their wagons began to arrive at the designated open area, just at the edge of town. Just seeing those colored wagons stirred a tremendous excitement within me. I spent each free moment at the circus site watching while the men marked the area for the tent and as equipment was being moved around. The big tent had been dragged over in sections. Two large poles were being placed underneath at the center and then pulled upright with the help of several horses. Once the center was raised, shorter poles were inserted around the outer portion of the tent, and soon it was easy to see the actual size. Men in pairs would then hammer long steel pegs around the outside, using their large sledgehammers in an alternating motion before moving on to the next position.

Watching this whole set-up process fascinated me and I was amazed that everybody seemed to know exactly what to do without much communication between them. Hours before the first scheduled performance, everything seemed to be completed. A special entrance tent had been added and over it was the name of the circus with light bulbs surrounding it. Little flags had been placed everywhere, which made it appear even more alive. Now my question was where I would get the money to see the show, and I knew that Mom would not be able to pay for us. The first matinee for children at a special price would be the next day. What to do?

Grandma would have to be my savior once again. Rather than asking her directly, I told her all about the upcoming matinee and that

82

all my friends were going. After some hesitation, she quietly gave me the necessary money to go. I realized that it was hard for her as well to make ends meet. Several of the boys from our neighborhood had arrived well in advance. It was important to secure a good seat for this exciting event. Overnight, an additional smaller tent had been set up for the animals, and they could be seen for an additional fee. Finally the main entrance was opened and everybody going to see the show began to rush toward it.

Simple bench-type bleachers surrounded the center ring. Above the entrance opposite the performers, in an enclosed square, was a four-man band in colorful outfits. After a few minutes of preparation, the band began to play and bright lights began to shine on the center as the ringmaster entered the arena. The show was truly exciting to see. Horses and elephants, monkeys and dogs, clowns and artists performed while the band played to each act. The whole new atmosphere of the tent, the wagons in which the circus people lived, the strange animals, and the performers fascinated me. I already looked forward to next year's event.

* * *

As life was beginning to look more hopeful for the future, so were the hopes of many for the return of their husbands, fathers, sons, and brothers. The war had been over for more than three years and most prisoners held by the Allied forces had been able to return home by now. Those held in Russian prisons and other places, like Dad, remained captive. For those relatives whose men had been reported as missing in action, hope was fading, although many still searched for missing relatives. Mom was receiving an occasional letter from Dad through the Red Cross, so we were at least assured that he was still alive.

The horrible stories of the last days of the fight at Stalingrad were now being brought by radio in a series of several weeks, and we came to learn about the horrors of the war that had taken place there. Of course we learned about the brutality of the war as it was perceived by the German soldiers and observers who fought there. In the evening we often talked about what Dad may have gone through and what his prison conditions might be like. Then the topic would usually change and Grandma would tell us Dad's growing up stories once again.

Wolfgang was nearly eight now and Marlene already six. Since Gunter was fourteen, he had some memory of Dad, but the rest of us children had to rely on his older pictures. It was probably hardest for Mom, having to be both parents all these difficult years. As we were getting older and growing, so was our need for more food, something food rations did not take into account. Clothing would usually be passed on from the oldest to the next in line. I never did mind this arrangement or receiving the things Gunter had outgrown.

While playing during the warm summer months, we would usually just wear a pair of shorts that was held up by suspenders over our bare shoulders. As each of us only had one pair of shoes, these had to be preserved, so we would run about in our wooden footwear consisting of a wooden contoured sole with a single strap across the front of the foot, a previous wartime issue. While walking or running on our cobblestone sidewalks, the noise generated by this footwear would echo in the narrow streets and made a quiet approach impossible.

Most of the clothing we had was made by Mom on her foot-operated sewing machine. It was usually done after we had all gone to bed. For my first communion, she had made me a short pants suit out of a white bed sheet for lack of other material.

Aunt Mary and her two daughters, Helga and Brigitte, were still living in the same house with us. Mom and Aunt Mary supported each other and were very close. Uncle Paul, Aunt Mary's husband, was also still held as prisoner of war and so both women shared the same predicament. Having them living in the same house was truly a blessing for all of us. As I recall, Aunt Mary's being so talkative and upbeat helped us, especially so during the frightening wartime period. She would often begin a sentence in a normal tone, but while continuing, her voice began to take on a higher pitch and, together with a laugh, she would almost run out of breath. We usually attributed her more outgoing personality as being that of a city person. Although she and her daughters had been living with us for several years now, she would often express her desire to return home to her city of Hannover.

One of the many food shortages were fresh fruits. Unless one had their own fruit trees or knew someone who would share them, these were much sought after. Most major roads between towns were lined with various fruit trees but were always off-limits and usually guarded. Once the fruit had ripened, each tree was then auctioned to the highest bidder for its harvest only. We boys would occasionally wander along those roads, and while assuring ourselves that no one was around to watch, we began throwing sticks into the branches until a desired amount of apples would drop for us to eat right on the spot.

One night during fall, after all of us children had already gone to bed, Mom and Aunt Mary decided to go out to get some apples for our families. Both equipped with a rucksack, they walked through the forest to a neighboring town to collect the fallen apples by the roadside, while always fearing being caught. Once they had collected a sufficient amount to fill their packs, they made their several-mile journey through the dark forest back home, hoping not to be intercepted by someone along the way. Relieved not to have been caught, they arrived back home before daybreak. Needless to say, for us, seeing all those apples the next morning was a joyful sight.

Mom was pleased that she would now have apples for us that would last us through the winter. For lack of storage, she laid them out on the floor underneath the bed in an unheated bedroom. Gunter and I, who shared that bedroom, soon found an apple to be a tasty late-evening snack. To avoid Mom noticing our occasional indulgence, we would always take an apple from the back to keep the front row intact. At Christmastime, when finally she tried to retrieve enough apples for each of our cookie plates, all she found was a single front row with a lot of dried-up apple cores behind them. Since there was little doubt about who the guilty ones were, Mom was upset at Gunter and myself, but in view of Christmas she quickly overcame her anger with us. We would often talk about this disappearing apple story in the years to follow, and it would always bring out a chuckle from the listeners.

* * *

A Local Jewish Cemetery

During the early part of summer in 1948, our town swimming pool, located about one kilometer outside of town, was reopened after years of dormancy. It was an old pool and its concrete walls had been patched in many places. The grass surrounding the pool was mowed and it gave the area a neater appearance. Two small barrack-type buildings served as a changing facility. Although it was old and barely made functional, for us this was paradise where we spent nearly every afternoon during the warm summer months.

The dirt country road leading to the pool was lined with fruit trees and it eventually turned into a narrow walkway among open fields. Near the end of this path and just prior to reaching the pool area, the narrow walkway began to drop off at a steep decline. From up on top, one could look down on the pool area, which was surrounded by bushes and a partially rusted section of wire fence.

Just before starting the decline, we had to pass a small abandoned Judenfriedhof (a Jewish cemetery) located just about one hundred feet to the left. Occasionally we would stop to read the leaning headstones of those buried beneath them. Most of them had become nearly impossible to read, as the stones had aged over the years of neglect. At times we tried to trace the inscriptions with our fingers in hope of trying to identify the letters and their meaning. It was puzzling to us why this little cemetery had been so neglected, since both of our town cemeteries were always so well cared for. Traditionally relatives felt obligated to maintain the graves of their deceased and did so on an almost daily basis. Not to do so would be considered shameful by the community.

In trying to answer our own question, we had come to realize that none of us boys had ever met a Jewish person. There were no relatives living here to take care of their graves. We had heard that those Jewish people who had lived here had sold their businesses to some locals prior to the war and had moved away. It was a subject that was rarely talked about, something we as children assumed was normal. We had overheard from the adults that the small grocery store across the street had once belonged to a Jewish person. He had, however, sold it to its current owner years before the war and had left Germany. On those rare occasion when Mom and Aunt Mary talked about this issue, Mom would usually shake her head while looking down at the mention of the awful years of the Juden verhaftungen (the arrests of the Jews).

She would then recall her own brother-in-law, who had remarried after her sister had died. His new wife had been arrested by the Gestapo, the secret police of the Nazi regime, for belonging to a Catholic women's league within the Christian Center Party. She was held in a prison camp in Lamsdorf, in the former German part of Schlesingen. Mom recalled those occasions when she would visit her outside the gate of the camp. How the poor hungry people behind the iron bars were begging those outside to bring them food. Soon even this was changed and a new barrier was erected inside the compound to prevent those incarcerated from approaching the gate, and so no more food could be passed on to them. Sometime later, the daughter of the incarcerated woman was arrested as well, and both mother and daughter ultimately perished while imprisoned. When Mom talked about these events, her face would take on a painful look and she would briefly shake her head as if to dispel these memories from her mind.

After the war, several barracks had been discovered in the distant forest. They had been kept secret until the end of the war. Even those in nearby towns had not been aware of the existence of these buildings. People now quietly speculated about their original use, although their real purpose was never revealed. For us boys it became something worth investigating, and so we made the long journey on foot to see for ourselves. Finally seeing the two simple barracks in the woods, some distance from any main road, left us wondering and speculating about the little we had heard from the adults.

The many atrocities that now came to be known left an impression on our young minds, although we did not fully understand then. For us it did not explain why people had been persecuted for so many years. Nor did we really understand the concept and purpose of the concentration camps. It had become a subject that was rarely talked about, and it was only with time and age that we would come to learn the truth about this dark period in history. For our young generation, it became a question of whether we had inherited the shame of the nation. As for me, this question would remain unanswered.

* * *

Mom's Sudden Illness

The later part of August 1948 was going to be a new trial for our family. It was around three o'clock on a weekday afternoon when I was called by someone to come into the house. As I entered through the kitchen door, I could see straight into our small living room. There in the middle of the room stood our town nurse indicating for me to come in. Although she displayed a gentle smile, I realized that something was seriously wrong. Upon entering, I immediately noticed Mom lying on the couch and looking very ill. "Your mom will have to go to the hospital," the nurse said while indicating for me to go up to the couch. While she slowly turned her head in my direction, I could see that Mom had cried. She looked at me and said my name with a very weak voice, holding her hand out for mine. I was so overcome with fear that I couldn't speak. The nurse then indicated for me to go back into the kitchen.

Gunter was standing in the kitchen and with the exception of me asking, "What is wrong with Mom?" we were both unable to speak. Aunt Mary had already taken care of Wolfgang and Marlene and so they were no longer in the same rooms.

Within minutes, two ambulance personnel carrying a stretcher came rushing through the kitchen and into the living room. About a minute later, they came back out carrying Mom. They briefly stopped on their way out as Mom just looked at us both, saying each of our names once again. Her voice was hardly audible and she appeared very weak. Then they moved on, carrying her to the waiting ambulance that would take her to the city hospital in Alfeld. Gunter walked out after them and I remained alone in the kitchen and began to cry. Many things began racing through my mind. I was worried about what would happen to Mom and for the first time I worried about what we would do without her.

Although she was petite, she had always seemed strong. Her moves and walk were always faster than the normal speed. Even while going across the street to the little grocery store, her walk was usually in double time. It was in her nature to move quickly, and having to provide for four children as a single parent gave her little time to rest. She had been mother and father for us all our lives. As children, we were usually absorbed in our own little world and accepted our lives as normal. Suddenly there was this reality and fear of her not being there. My thoughts went back to the many nightly bomb raids when she would be the last, double timing with her two big suitcases, which always seemed far too heavy for her. How much safer we felt under her arms while destruction overhead threatened our survival. Even at my young age of nine and a half, I had come to realize how much we had relied on her strength.

Mrs. Schaper, a local woman, came to cook and stay with us. Grandma helped as much as she could and she now became our closest relative, which gave us some comfort. Mrs. Schaper was a woman with no patience and we quickly learned that it was best not to question her or disobey her. This, however, made us miss Mom all the more. Although we were not able to visit her in the city hospital, we were told that Mom had kidney stone problems, something we did not understand. She was supposed to be getting better and could be released to come home soon.

Mom remained in the hospital for well over a week before she was able to return home. Although she was not able to do any strenuous work for a while, to us, at least she was home. And so life slowly returned to normal. With Dad having been away all these years, Mom was all the parent we knew, so her absence had really shaken us. Although Wolfgang was usually the one who had the greatest need for her, we were all grateful to have her back and promised to help more with the daily chores.

By the time summer was coming to an end, Mom had recovered and was back in her daily routine of cooking and washing and caring for the family. Early fall always meant more work and less time for play. Wood needed to be split and stacked. Coal had to be purchased and stacked, which was always a dirty job. The hardest task for us was harvesting potatoes, as this required several afternoons and the involvement of the whole family. Even Wolfgang and Marlene were able to collect potatoes off the ground after they had been dug up.

The most distasteful fall activity for us, however, was emptying out the underground liquid manure tank, which contained human and animal waste products. This was done by lowering a bucket into the tank and, once filled, raising it and then pouring it into a large barrel resting on a hand-pulled wagon. Once the barrel was filled, it was taken outside of town and spread on gardens and fields as fertilizer. I was never quite sure what I dreaded more: the smell associated with this task or the embarrassment of pulling the stinky wagon through town. Now that I had begun to take notice of girls, to be seen doing this task felt quite degrading and embarrassing.

* * *

Return of the Gypsies

As children we had heard about Gypsies as being people who were nearly always on the move. Somehow they enjoyed a special status as wandering people and had the freedom to move around most European countries without any restrictions. It was not clear why that was so, but then, as children we had little concerns for political decisions unless they affected us directly. Someone had mentioned that Gypsies had not been in Germany for a number of years but we assumed that during the war many people were unable to travel, and we simply accepted that as the reason. Now they were again traveling freely throughout the country, and this would be our first encounter with them. We had been told by some of the elders that Gypsies would steal young children, but so far we had not ever seen anyone place a lot of trust in this old belief.

On this early fall day of 1948 several of the people who had arrived on the bus from the nearby city of Alfeld had seen eight to ten Gypsy wagons along the highway. It was estimated that they would be coming through town within just a few hours. In addition to the idea of stealing children, people now voiced concerns that Gypsies also had a reputation for stealing in general, and so people began to take certain precautions by closing gates and doors. As expected, by late afternoon the first wagon came into sight, coming down the main route, heading north, and directly passing by our house. Gunter, Wolfgang, Marlene, and I, together with two of our neighboring boys, moved behind the fence and so were securely in our own yard.

Soon the first completely enclosed wooden wagon approached us, and it would soon be passing our yard. The wagon was painted quite colorfully; and the others, though still some distance from us, had a similar appearance, something Gypsies were known for. Each of the wagons was pulled by a team of two horses. A man who appeared to be older and possibly the father of a family sat proudly on the front bench holding the rein and directing his team. His clothing, too, was quite colorful and fit the wagon he was riding on. His complexion was darker than we were used to seeing and similar to a dark suntan. His hair was black and matched his other features. As he began to pass by, he briefly looked toward us, catching us staring at him. As we were quite close at that moment, we could see his dark eyes looking at us.

From behind the windows of the passing wagon, several children with features similar to those of the driver were looking at us. Walking at the rear was a woman in a colorful blouse and a floor-length skirt. Her hair, too, was black, wavy, and shoulder length. She had the same dark eyes and complexion.

Eight additional wagons passed by our secure location. Some of the men were walking by the side but near the front of their wagons while holding the rein. The people passing us were similar in appearance. With the exception of an occasional glance, they seemed to show little reaction toward all the onlookers staring at them. What amazed us most were the many children we noticed behind each window, and we began to wonder if perhaps any of them had been stolen from their real parents. They, contrary to their adults, seemed to be as interested in looking at us as we were in them. I couldn't help but feel a little sorry for them for reasons I was unsure of.

Their appearance, while similar between them, was quite different from us. Yet there was a pride that was quite noticeable. I began to visualize them playing their music while sitting around their campfires in the evening, as had been often described to us. Many questions arose within me. Where were they going? Did it really matter? How did they get their food? Do the children have to go to school? What happens when one of the horses gets sick? Germans were so used to schedules and order, and so this lifestyle of the Gypsies was hard to understand.

The next morning we learned that the nine wagons with their families had camped just outside of town. They had allowed their horses to graze freely in the farmers' not-yet-harvested oat fields. This of course had several of the local farmers angry, but without much recourse since the violators had since moved on. Additionally there was concern that items may have disappeared during the course of the night, which was suspected when such groups decided to camp nearby.

Although this was our first encounter with traveling Gypsies, other groups would occasionally come through town in larger and smaller groups. I was always eager to watch them, and even though I did not understand the desire for their lifestyle, I couldn't help but admire the freedom they must have felt.

* * *

Dad's Homecoming

In late January 1949 the war had been over for nearly four years. It had not been a particularly harsh winter so far. Gunter and I had been out sledding part of the afternoon. It was nearly five o'clock and already dark and time for us to go home, which was only a few houses down the street. Once inside, we removed our rubber boots and jackets in the hallway. Mom always had a fire in the kitchen stove and the warmth felt really good. Supper would not be until six and so we had time to do our homework for school. Wolfgang, who was going on eight, and Marlene, about six, were playing in the small living room next to the kitchen. There was an open door connecting both rooms. In three months, I was going to be ten and so I felt somewhat privileged to be part of the older boys' group.

Aunt Mary, who lived just across from our kitchen, was talking with Mom. She usually came across the hall many times during the day and so it had become a routine that we accepted as quite normal. She was just about to leave to go back to her place, so I could concentrate on my homework. I always liked her visits as she enjoyed talking and laughing. I think it helped all of us just being around her. "Oh God!" she exclaimed while looking at our kitchen clock. "Anna, I have to make supper for the girls." And with that she turned toward the door.

In the meantime, I had opened my math book to our assignment, when we were interrupted by a firm knock at our kitchen door. All of us immediately looked in the direction of the door. Aunt Mary, who was just about to grab for the doorknob, jumped back in surprise.

95

Mom quickly acknowledged with a "Come in." The door opened and we recognized our local mail carrier. He came through the door and his hand went to the visor of his mail carrier hat as a sign of greeting. Mail was delivered around noon each day and so his appearance was quite surprising. There was a tense moment as he passed a piece of paper to Mom while advising her that it was a telegram from the Red Cross. She nervously reached for it, and breaking the seal with her thumb, she unfolded it.

The mail carrier was still standing there but all attention was now on Mom staring at the telegram. As telegrams were usually known to convey bad news, these were truly tense seconds for all in the room. Wolfgang and Marlene had by now rushed into the kitchen to see what was going on. Almost instantly Mom's face changed from a worried look to a happy smile, and we realized that it must be good news. She then read the message aloud: "Coming home today, Georg!"

"Dad is coming home" was our immediate response, and suddenly the peaceful scene had changed into a joyful shouting. Doors flung open in response to the sudden commotion, and quickly everybody in the house was gathered in the hall. The news quickly reached the neighbors and more people filled the narrow hallway. "When is he arriving?" someone asked, trying to be heard over the excited chatter. There was a short quiet. "The next train should be arriving from Voldagsen at six, in less then fifteen minutes," someone shouted over the excitement in the room. Voldagsen was the national railway station that connected with our local train. "We are going to the train station to see if he is arriving" was Gunter's response as he looked at Mom. She just nodded, and with that we quickly got into our boots and coats and ran out the door. Our neighbor's daughter, Liesel, had joined Gunter and myself, and we were now running toward the station, about a half kilometer away.

Coming around the corner onto the Bahnhofstrasse (Station Street), we could hear that the train had already arrived at our small station. The coal-filled smoke from the locomotive reached our nostrils as we got closer. Doors to the railcars were still being slammed and the locomotive was giving off the familiar frequent burst of steam. While still running through the dark, we could hear the voices of the passengers now exiting the station and coming toward us. How were we going to recognize him in this darkness? We slowed down to a walk. Suddenly, in her excitement, Liesel began to shout "Herr Bonisch, Herr Bonisch!" as we had now come to a halt.

"Maybe he is on the next train," Gunter interjected while listening for a response from the passengers. Liesel continued to shout, when suddenly out of the dark a deep voice answered, "Here." We immediately ran in the direction of the voice, and Liesel continued to shout "Herr Bonisch" until we were suddenly in front of a tall man carrying a large suitcase.

I recall saying "Papa?" in a questioning voice. "Is that Manfred?" he asked in a deep voice. Holding out my hand, he took it and with the other he gently pressed me against himself in a hugging fashion. In the darkness, I really could not make out his face, but that would soon change. He then took Gunter's hand and, bending down, ran his other hand over my brother's hair. "This is Liesel, our neighbor," Gunter said, pointing in her direction, and he shook her hand as well. "They are waiting for your arrival at home" was all I could say. Dad picked up his suitcase, while taking my hand in the other, and we began walking. All three of us tried to tell him that we had just received his telegram and immediately ran toward the station to meet him, even though we didn't know when he would be arriving.

Although many things were said as we walked to the house, I was so elated by hearing his deep voice that I only recall bits of the conversation. Liesel ran ahead the last hundred meters to announce his arrival. In my excitement, I was tempted to do the same, but at the same time did not want to let go of his strong hand. As we entered the house, coming into the dimly lit hall, the kitchen door was wide open and Mom was standing in the middle of the room. The brighter kitchen light enhanced her small figure. She had one arm around Marlene, who was right next to her in anticipation. There was a brief moment of silence as Dad set down his suitcase. I had let go of his hand and run ahead of him into the hall so that I could fully enjoy seeing him come into the light.

He then quickly walked over to Mom and they hugged for what seemed to us a long time. I recall Mom saying "Georgel" and Dad saying "Annel" while they were embracing. I realized that by adding the *l* to each other's names was their expression of affection. How long we had waited for and talked about this very moment. He then picked up Marlene, and while he talked to her, she looked somewhat puzzled at the man with the deep voice. Setting her back down, he turned to Wolfgang, who had partially hid himself behind Mom and didn't seem sure whether to shake Dad's hand. Oma, as we called Grandma, was next in line to greet her son with tears flowing down her cheeks. Others in the hallway now eagerly approached him, trying to shake his hand and welcoming him home. Additional neighbors began to arrive to welcome Dad back after so many years of being away.

I stood to the side and in the kitchen light I could now see that he was quite tall, especially next to Mom. Although his hairline was receding, his hair was a dark blond. His face seemed thin and his cheeks were sunken inward, causing his cheekbones to stand out. He had a gentle face and maintained a friendly smile throughout the evening, which lasted until late into the night. Someone had brought some beer and most had crowded into the small living room, while others stationed themselves under the door frame and even in the kitchen. Everybody was eager to hear about his years of imprisonment and how he had become a prisoner of war.

All of his stories fascinated me as I quietly listened and tried to visualize the events he described. One story in particular drew my special attention. He told about the time he and one other German soldier and a nurse escaped from their prison compound in Yugoslavia. While being in this prison camp, all the prisoners would be called out daily to stand in formation and at attention. One of the Yugoslav officers would then go through the rows to point out numerous individuals who would be transported to a different location. This would continue for several days, with additional prisoners being called out to be transported away.

On one of the following days, a special work detail was selected and also driven away. Each had been given a shovel and so it was expected that they would be doing some form of ground work. Once they arrived, they began to see that their comrades who had been taken away previously had been shot and it was now their duty to bury them. This shocking news created much fear in the camp and so Dad and a fellow prisoner decided to escape. Once they were ready, they watched while two guards moved in opposite directions, and under the cover of darkness, they slipped through and under the wire, taking a German nurse with them. They traveled all night and rested in forests during the day.

Then they came upon the river Drau, which they had to cross. Stripping and carrying their belongings overhead, they attempted to swim across. This created a problem, as the nurse was not so willing to undress and to follow the men in their attempt to cross this river. After some convincing, she agreed and they finally were able to get to the other side.

After several more nights of traveling in this manner, they reached Austria, to the north. From the edge of a forest, they could see a distant prison camp operated by British troops. It seemed that the many German prisoners were able to move around freely. Upon watching this camp for some time and being driven by hunger, they finally decided that it must be safe to approach this facility. As expected, they were fed and allowed to move around freely.

After three days, Dad and his comrades decided to move on through Austria and into Germany. The war had been over for a year and so this seemed the practical thing to do. On the morning of their intended departure, the prison was suddenly guarded and all were instructed to line up. They were asked from where they had escaped, as nearly all of them were German escapees. They were then loaded on guarded trucks and buses and subsequently driven back to their original prison camp. Only the nurse who had escaped with them was allowed to return to Germany, and so ended their few days of freedom. I couldn't help but think how frustrating it must have been for them to come so close, only to be returned for several more years of prison.

It was his stories and his deep voice that kept my attention until late into the night. I got up early the next morning so that I could see Dad when he got up. It was a new experience to finally have the father we had been waiting for all these years. The memories of that morning are very special, as I watched him prepare to shave. Sitting at the kitchen table, he began to lather his face, while at the same time talking to me. I don't recall so much about what was said. Instead I listened to the sound of the razor as it went across his lower face, removing both shaving cream and his beard. Watching this masculine event while hearing his deep voice filled me with an enormous feeling of peace and security that I will never forget.

People continued to stop in during the next several days to welcome Dad home and hear about his time away. We adjusted quickly to having him home, and it was a special treat to have him at the table during our mealtimes. This was also the time when we would ask him to tell us his war stories, which we were willing to hear over and over again. Many other families were still waiting for the return of their men and so we felt very blessed to have Dad finally with us. We children now had our father; however, for Mom it meant that she now had a shoulder to lean on and someone to help with the hard work she had had to carry nearly alone for so long.

Perhaps it was my own imagination, but somehow I felt more drawn to Dad than my brothers or sister. Just being near him, hearing his voice, or just him clearing his throat, or the smell of his pipe was reassuring to me. Even during the nighttime, I began to feel more at peace just to know that he was in the house with us. He soon began working again as carpenter and cabinetmaker in the nearby factory, and so life took on a new routine for us.

Over the next weeks and months, I came to appreciate Dad as a good father. One outstanding quality about him was his love of people. He quickly came to know them and would greet nearly everyone with a warm smile. He would often have old friends visit. They would sit chatting until late into the night. Just being allowed to stay in their company was a real treat for us children then. Seeing Mom and Dad now enjoying the frequent company of their friends brought with it a new vitality for all of us.

Our friends Jurgen and Rudie from next door were now hoping that their dad would be released from his Russian prison soon. Our other neighbors across the yard, whose father had been missing in action, still had not received any more news. Mrs. Meyer would occasionally talk with Mom about her missing husband and was losing hope of ever seeing him again. Four years had passed since the end of the war and her question seemed to be, when does one finally accept that he is dead? Most prisoners held by the Russians had not been able to come home yet, and so there always remained that tiny hope of a miracle. Someone returning home might possibly provide the answer that he was either killed in action or had been a fellow prisoner. Occasionally it was reported that someone returned home after having been a prisoner of war or having been declared dead.

That same year the town offered land the size of a normal garden lot. Since the entire area had previously been land overgrown with trees and shrubs as well as all sorts of weeds, the new owners were now required to cultivate their lots. The thought of owning such a lot was quite exciting for us, until we finally saw the sector allotted to us.

Our land parcel was covered by numerous tree stumps and large craters, and we were uncertain whether the craters had been left from previously removed tree trunks or had been created by bombs. Mom would come out in the afternoon to bring us food and something to drink, and it was these breaks that I cherished and that had now set me apart as an official male member of the family.

For Gunter and me, it was an opportunity to work with Dad to clear the assigned area. It was extremely hard work, especially for Dad. Seeing it finally turning into a workable garden gave us all a great deal of pride. It would not be until the following season that we could claim our first harvest of potatoes and other vegetables. We would often talk about how we had worked together to cultivate this piece of property. For me, it was the working together that made it something special and unforgettable.

During one of those fall afternoons, Dad collapsed on the living room floor. With the help of Mom, Gunter, and myself, we were able to carry him to the nearby couch. Shortly thereafter, his temperature began to rise and he started to shake violently without ever showing any signs of consciousness. Mom then advised us that Dad was having a malaria attack, something he had contracted in one of the Balkan states during the war. Mom began to cover him with blankets to keep him warm, and it wasn't until the next day that he began to show signs of relaxing.

This sudden attack was quite severe and would require two additional days of rest before he was able to get up and move around. For us to see him suddenly in such a vulnerable state of total disability was both frightening and choking. After all, it was the sound of his voice and his strength that I had admired so much. Following his three-day disability, he slowly began to follow his daily routine and things began to return to normal.

Dad had been back about a year now and how quickly we had gotten used to having him at home. It was now early 1950 and more of the surviving prisoners of war were returning home. These were mainly those soldiers kept in Russian prisons. Jurgen and Rudie from next door were hoping their father would be one of those to be released soon. Their mother and ours had become good neighbors over the many years during and after the war, and they often talked about their similar family struggles. As it was often the case in Germany, they always addressed each other as missus and used their family names, so they never got on a first-name basis.

Then one day, Jurgen and Rudie's father came home and again there was rejoicing in the neighborhood. Of course, all of us children wanted to see him as quickly as possible to see what a man released from Russian prison looked like. He too was quite thin looking, but he had an almost permanent, gentle smile. He was originally born in town and usually spoke in the old Duinger dialect. He and Dad soon became good friends, as they had many hard stories to share.

By now the Meyers, our other neighbors across the yard, had given up hope of their husband and father still being alive. Although Heinz and Carl were part of our boys' group, we usually did not talk about it. Neither of the boys had really known their father and so their Mom too had taken the place of both parents, as all of our mothers had during those difficult years.

* * *

An Excitable Cow

Often when there was nothing else to do, I just liked to hang out with my older brother, Gunter, who usually sooner or later came up with ideas to entertain us. So I recall one warm summer afternoon about mid August. It was harvest time and the beginning of the busiest period for the local farmers. Farmers would ride their empty wagons, pulled by a team of horses, heading out of town to their various fields. Here they would load up their wagons as high as they possibly could and then return back to town and their farms for unloading. Since we had nearly eight to ten farms inside the town, the movements of farm wagons were quite frequent at this time of year. Since nearly all of this was done with the use of horses, there was a certain pace about this scene that I found relaxing to watch.

This afternoon, Gunter and I were standing on the sidewalk with our backs leaned against the wall of the shoemaker's shop next door. On warm days such as this, the shop door was usually wide open, and a faint smell of leather and glue permeated the air. This very familiar smell, along with the sound of the frequent hammering from inside the shop, was somehow quite soothing. It seemed at that moment as if time had stood still and we were able to experience our surroundings as people had enjoyed doing a hundred years before. However, this peaceful scene was about to change.

From our position, we could see up and down the main road, and were close to where the Triftstrasse merged with the Hauptstrasse. This was the center of town, where most of the daily activity occurred. The time was probably around five in the afternoon, something we were not too concerned about that day. The sun was still high and it was a clear and warm day. Other than the periodic farm wagons and an occasional car or truck, there was little activity. There was Herr Bergmann, our grade school principal, just coming around the corner on the sidewalk opposite ours. We looked at him for a brief moment as he walked erect while swinging his cane with every other step. "Let's go around the corner so we don't have to greet him," Gunter said, already moving in that direction. Once he had passed, we returned to our previous location.

We had taken our old position when we noticed Herr Muller sitting in his wooden hay wagon, being pulled by a cow. He was one of the smallest farmers in town, and since he did not have a horse, he did all his work with his few cows. He had finished turning onto the main road and was now slowly heading in our direction. We knew this as his daily routine, as he picked up freshly cut grass or hay from his field outside of town, which was needed to feed his cows and goat. Since we saw him almost daily during the summer months, I paid little attention to this slow-moving scene.

Herr Muller, while sitting on the grass in his wagon, seemed quite content with the speed as he was holding the rein loosely in his hands, allowing the cow to set her own pace. She obviously knew her way home and so the slowly approaching scene seemed to fit the lazy day. The cow was now about thirty feet away when Gunter, now standing upright, suddenly said, "Watch this," and with his hands outstretched as if to milk the cow, he crossed the street heading straight for the unsuspecting animal. Before I could realize what he was trying to do, the cow took a sudden leap forward, lifting its front legs high into the air as it was held back by the wagon attached behind it. As the front legs landed back on the cobblestone street, she yanked forward and quickly turned into a fast running pace, hauling the wagon with its surprised passenger behind her.

The surprised Herr Muller jumped up in the wagon, trying to control the wild, running cow with his reins, but without success. The animal kept running until it was out of sight, and before I could comprehend what had happened, the whole thing was over. I looked at Gunter, who was now returning from his stunt with a grin of satisfaction. Several of the nearby townspeople who had seen the commotion were still staring at us, probably questioning what had just upset the cow. "How did you know that the cow would react like that?" I asked, still somewhat surprised.

"I didn't. I just wanted to see how she would react when I did that," was his proud reply.

"Wow, that sure was exciting" was all I could say while still trying to visualize the whole event.

This whole event played out again and again in my mind during the rest of the evening. Before going to sleep that night, I made up my mind that I would try to impress my younger brother, Wolfgang, with the same event tomorrow afternoon.

The following day began slightly overcast, but by late morning it began to clear and by afternoon it had turned into a beautiful summer day. At lunch I advised Wolfgang that I would show him something special later that day. His response was only a questionable look. He was eight years old and usually enjoyed it when he was included in anything we did, so he was easily persuaded by an older brother of eleven. The afternoon seemed to go by slowly as I anticipated a repeat of yesterday's event. To be sure not to miss the farmer's daily return, we positioned ourselves again outside the shoe repair shop at about half past four. While waiting anxiously, I practiced my approach to the cow mentally to be sure that I could repeat Gunter's performance exactly. In my own excitement, I kept telling Wolfgang how he was going to like what he was about to see.

From the chime of the church tower I knew that it was now a quarter till five, and so we had waited about fifteen minutes. I kept staring expectantly at the intersection, waiting for the cow and cart to make its way around the corner. Another five minutes passed and it should be any second before the cow would come into sight. I turned to Wolfgang to tell him once again to watch me. Concentrating while expectantly looking back toward the intersection, I nervously waited. "There!" was all I could say as the head and body of the cow slowly appeared around the corner. Herr Muller was again in his usual position, sitting on top of the grass in his wagon. I was now nervously preparing for my move. Moving too soon could spoil the whole thing. The cow was now about thirty feet away and I could see Herr Muller looking at us.

"Watch this" were my last words as I started to walk toward the unsuspecting animal with my hands held out, as Gunter had done the day before. Suddenly, even before I expected any reaction, the cow jumped and leaped forward at a quick running pace. At this moment, I could see Herr Muller jumping off the wagon. He just missed being run over by his own wagon. He landed on his feet while bracing himself with his right hand on the ground to prevent from falling onto his side. He quickly recovered himself and was now beginning to rush toward me. The cow was still running down the street totally out of control, and my immediate realization was now that he had abandoned his wagon and cow to come after me. It was not supposed to happen this way. Fear gripped me and I turned to run.

"He is old and will not be able to catch me. He will soon give up" were my thoughts as I began to run into the nearby farmyard. Even while running, I had noticed people staring at us. I was now nearly across the yard and quickly turned back only to see Herr Muller still running after me. The barn door was open at both ends and so I turned from the yard and ran through the open barn. From the running sound coming off the concrete floor, I could tell that he was still behind me. Coming out at the other side, I again made my way across the yard and through the stables, as this was familiar territory for me. "He will soon have to give up" was my thought now, mixed with fear. Coming out of the stables and running across the yard once again, I began to realize that if he didn't catch me now he would probably complain to my father, and that would be bad news.

I was now again aiming for the open barn, trying to decide what to do. Realizing that he was not about to give up, I began to slow my running pace, allowing him to catch up to me. I had come to the quick realization that it was best to take my punishment here and now. As I slowed down, he seized me from behind and, grabbing my shirt, yanked me to a stop and immediately began to beat on me. As my back was toward him, the impacts were mainly on my neck and shoulders. My head was tucked into my shoulders and I leaned forward, so my hands came up, shielding the back of my neck. I didn't dare look at him for fear that it would evoke further anger. I tried not to resist and in doing so hoped for a quick ending to this embarrassing beating. As his blows appeared to slow down, I could hear him grumbling something I didn't attempt to understand.

As he finally released me, I began to straighten up, still looking at the barn floor, as it was too humiliating even now to look at him directly. From the side of my eyes, I could see his hand waving with the index finger pointing up. It seemed that he was now calming down, as his voice became clearer, but he was still shaking that index finger at me—this time low enough so that I could clearly see it. I slowly began to look at him and just realized how short he was. "Don't ever try to scare my cow again or next time it will be worse," he said and slowly began to turn, taking his first steps away from me. I had seen his face for a brief moment and it didn't seem to have the anger I had expected. Perhaps the beating had relieved him of that.

As he walked toward the open door, I remained standing inside the barn while my thoughts were still racing and my hands still shaking. Watching him leave the barn, I noticed how bowlegged he walked and wondered how he was able to run so fast. Although I had just endured a beating, I was not in pain and somehow felt that I had gotten off easy. At this point, I began to think about a repercussion from Dad. Would Herr Muller stop at our house and tell him about this? I feared that Dad's punishment would be much harsher. As I slowly walked out onto the sidewalk, I could see Herr Muller walking toward his small farm house without stopping at ours. In spite of all that I had just received, I felt grateful to a man who had just chased me and had given me a deserved beating. Looking around, I realized that none of the people in the vicinity had witnessed my embarrassment since it had taken place inside the barn.

Wolfgang was now walking toward me with an expectant look. "Did he catch you and beat you?" was his immediate question. I only nodded my head in response, still somewhat embarrassed. "Wow, the cow sure ran all the way," he exclaimed without waiting for a further reply to his first question. "Herr Muller almost got run over by his own cow and wagon," he went on, still excited about all that he had just witnessed.

We both waited some time before we went home for supper. I made him promise not to say anything to our parents. I expected that they would have surely heard about it by now. It wasn't until several days later when the subject came up during dinner. When we finally talked about the event, it came across as rather funny. Even Mom and Dad couldn't help but smile and shake their heads. The fact that I had already received my punishment from Herr Muller seemed sufficient for Dad and no more was said about it.

I have met Herr Muller on numerous occasions later in life and found him to be a down-to-earth, decent man. On none of those occasions did he ever mention the incident again, for which I was quite grateful.

* * *

Our Growing Community

Many of the refugees who had come to live in our town became permanent residents. Their former German homeland was now annexed to Poland and so these refugees were no longer able to return to their homes and properties. The original way refugees had been looked upon by the locals slowly began to fade. Although the newcomers often spoke with different dialects, their daily association with others in town made this less of an issue. This permanency was further fostered through marriages with locals and the raising of their children together. It had expanded the population of the town by at least another thousand people and slowly enlarged the town through additional housing.

Changes were not only noticeable in terms of size but also through new traditions brought by these newcomers. Simple changes, such as different meals previously unknown in our area, became popular. The somewhat narrow thinking of our semi farm community took on a broader view of what occurred around them. As people talked about their lost homelands, we began to learn much from them.

By now our Catholic church community had also grown with this influx of people from predominantly Catholic areas. In addition to Mom, Dad had also become quite involved in our church, and so as children we were automatically drawn into those activities as well. Through this we formed many new friendships, not only in our town but with many Catholics from the surrounding towns as well. Our Sunday services were still conducted in our local Protestant church, where I also faithfully served as an altar boy.

Many of those in town who had been bombed out in nearby cities were slowly returning to them as new apartment buildings were made available. This desire to return was understandable, as most Germans continued to live their lives in or near the place of their birth. Aunt Mary and our two cousins also moved back to the city of Hannover, and although it freed up additional rooms for us, I was personally sad to see them leave.

With the influx of people from other parts of Germany, the dialect spoken by the original townspeople began to fade out. Even the older Duingers now made an effort to speak the more understandable High German that the nearby city of Hannover was famous for. Overcrowded housing also began to improve as new homes were slowly beginning to enlarge the town.

A Lesson in Pride

During one of our Sunday services, an announcement was made that a Catholic community from a city near the border of Holland, about a three-hundred-kilometer distance, was inviting children from our community for a three-month stay. This was also intended for those children going to make their first communion to do so in an almost completely Catholic environment. Since we were considered as part of the diaspora, this would provide an opportunity to attend a Catholic school, something not available in our own area. Those going would be staying with local Catholic families. I had already made my first communion the previous year and so it was uncertain whether I would qualify for this opportunity.

I was not quite sure why I was so anxious to go—whether it was the long train ride or just the whole idea of going someplace different. My younger brother, Wolfgang, had decided to go and after some convincing my parents agreed to allow me to go as well. The fact that I had already made my first communion didn't seem to be a problem for those who made the arrangements.

Approximately seven weeks later, about twenty-five of us children, both boys and girls, began the one-day train trip to our new community. At most major train stations along the way, Red Cross workers made sure that we were being transferred properly and provided us with sandwiches. After a full day's ride, we finally arrived at our destination late in the evening. While we were waiting inside the passenger waiting areas, the new foster parents arrived one by one to pick up their assigned children. Wolfgang had already been picked up and I recall being the last one still waiting. It was now getting serious, as the long-awaited train ride was over. Who would I be living with? How would I adapt to a new school? All these things were now racing through my mind, as there was no going back for the next three months.

Finally, a young man and woman walked into the area, and after briefly talking to the organizer, they came over to me. They then took me to their home, by bicycle, about a half a kilometer distance. Not much was said as both the young man and the young woman occasionally spoke to each other in the local dialect that was nearly impossible for me to understand. As we walked into the house, the family was sitting at supper. My new temporary parents introduced themselves as Herr and Frau Klein and Grandpa, who was sitting next to them. The young man and woman who had picked me up at the station were their older children. There were two additional sons, one of which seemed to be close to my age.

It was a tense evening as I sat down to have supper with my new family. Frau Klein was a heavy woman of medium height, and because of her weight she was not able to stand for any length of time. That evening a type of porridge was served; it was popular to that region, as I learned later, but unknown to me. It was mixed with plums that gave it a taste similar to the smell of vomit, and upon tasting it nearly caused me to throw up. Immediately after finishing supper, Frau Klein tapped the plate with her spoon as signal for the children to clear the table and wash the dishes. From her place at the table, she would shout her commands in her high-pitched voice, but she never involved herself in any of the housework.

In the days to follow, I learned that her interest was running her little grocery store on the ground floor of their modest house. Wednesdays and Saturdays she would sell her fruits and vegetables at the city market. Before too long, I too was required to call out to the names of fruits and vegetables to passing shoppers in hopes of attracting them to our stand. This activity seemed very natural for Frau Klein but always made me feel very self-conscious and uncomfortable. It took some time before I recognized that, although she was somewhat loud and commanding, she was by no means unkind. Herr Klein, on the other hand, was a quiet but kind man who usually did what he was told and never really said too much, as I recall. I soon began to understand why this family had volunteered to have me stay with them, as most of my time here was taken up with work.

The city itself still showed much of the destruction caused by the wartime bombing, even though the war had been over for about six years. In the process of rebuilding, occasional unexploded bombs were discovered below the rubble of fallen buildings. Wolfgang had been attached to a family who lived on the third floor of a partially bombed-out apartment building. It was the end section of the building that had remained and was now standing in an open area alone. One side consisted of a bare brick wall and had previously supported a stairway. One could easily see where the previous attached building had been torn away. The concrete entrance to a nearby air-raid shelter was a further reminder of this dark time.

Back home it was easier to forget this awful period we all had lived through. Here I was again reminded by seeing the still-existing destruction. I couldn't help but think of the fear families must have felt during those frequent day and night raids. With time I adjusted to these new surroundings and began to see them as normal.

Within just a few days, I had the opportunity to visit my brother and to meet his new family. Although they seemed to be people of little means, they appeared to be very kind. I was glad that he was staying with such good people, especially since it was his first time away from home. Although we were probably both homesick, I was not going to admit to it since I had insisted on coming here. For Wolfgang it was probably much harder being away from our parents and so being with a good family would help his adjustment.

Within two weeks of our arrival, summer vacation was over and we now started attending a Catholic school. By now the second-oldest son of the Kleins had taken me under his wing and trained me to do the daily housework together. He was also a scout leader and included me in his activities, which provided the occasional change and free time.

After completing our three-month stay, Wolfgang and I were glad to return home, where all our friends greeted us at the train station. Even then, I was too proud to tell my parents of my negative experiences, so I claimed to have had a great time. When the same family invited me again to come and stay with them the following year for an additional three months, I was too proud to admit my reluctance and so accepted and went. My stay there was much like the year before, with the exception that I was now more familiar with the daily routine. During my last month there, I contracted pneumonia and spent two weeks in the city hospital. I recall these two weeks as the best period of my stay with the Kleins.

I have often asked myself since, how I could have been so proud as to endure three more months of the same annoyance, especially since it was my choice, when all I had to say was "no thank you" instead. Perhaps it was a good disciplinary experience that would serve me later in life and help me to adapt to different circumstances.

* * *

New Friends from the East

As part of our growing Catholic community, Mom and Dad had become friends with Herr Koenig, a gentlemen slightly older than my parents. Since he lived by himself, he would often come to visit us. We all liked him and in a sort of way we looked at him as the grandfather we never really had. His son and his family lived in the eastern part of Germany occupied by the Russians and so he would rarely ever see them. Traveling to West Germany was extremely difficult and required authorization by the East German government. When such an authorization was granted, it was usually only given to one or two family members, while the rest had to remain behind. Those left behind became the assurance and so the hostages that the traveling members would return to their home in the east by a specified date.

The son of Herr Koenig had once visited his aging father and he too became friends with Dad. Although he had to report back to the local authorities in East Germany by a certain date, his plan was for his family to escape to the west. The plan was not without its dangers, as people were often killed while trying to escape the communist sector. He now had to carefully consider how to get a family of seven—a wife, four children, and a grandmother—across one of the world's most guarded and dangerous borders. This also meant leaving all their possessions behind, including a house, for a hope of a better life in the west.

A year had passed since his last visit to his father in the west, and so he now applied again for such an authorization. He also included one of his sons to travel with him to meet his aging grandfather. With many difficulties and the assurance that the majority of his family would remain in the east, he was finally given the travel permit, with his assurance to return by a certain date. Several days after both father and son had arrived in the west, they began to implement the next step. A local doctor willingly issued a written statement indicating that the father had become seriously ill and was unable to return home by the designated date. Under these circumstances, because they understood the conditions in the east, doctors in the west were usually willing to cooperate. Since this was done mainly for humanitarian reasons, helping someone from the other side was not seen as unethical.

The doctor's statement was sent to his wife in the east so that she then could apply for the authorization for her and the youngest daughter to visit their supposedly sick husband in the west. As this now reduced the remaining family to only two children and the grandmother, it became ever more difficult to obtain the required travel authorization.

After an additional statement from the same doctor pertaining to her husband's prolonged and worsening condition, she and her daughter were finally allowed to travel to the west. Again, this was only granted for a certain period of time, after which they had to return or the remaining family members would suffer the consequences.

Now that four of the seven family members had reached the west, it was certain that the remaining family members would be closely watched by the East German secret police, known as the FOPO. They now had become hostages without any special confinement. Could they possibly succeed three times in a row and outsmart a very devious and dangerous government security system? Any attempt to leave would mean a sure arrest and would force the other family members to return.

Hearing Dad and Herr Koenig frequently discuss this extremely dangerous attempt caused me to realize what risk this family was really taking. From their conversations, I began to learn what it really was that they were trying to escape from. We in the west were free to move around. This was not so in the eastern part, where the government first had to authorize any form of travel. Their life-threatening risk was to live in freedom, which we already took for granted. Although we had heard much about the horrors in the Soviet-occupied section of

Germany, being privileged to this secret about the dangerous attempt to escape made us feel that we were a part of their lives as well as their fears.

It was now their grandma's turn to try to outsmart the system, and there would be no second chance if caught. Time was also a factor, as it had to be accomplished within the period of the valid travel visa by the mother and daughter. Confiding in anyone about such an attempt was too risky. This included the children, who would only be told at the last moment prior to leaving. To escape without getting caught, Grandma and the two boys had to secretly get to Berlin, a city that was partly under Russian occupation and was blocked off from the western sector of the city.

To avoid being obvious, they left their house during the night, leaving just a few lights burning to give any passersby the appearance that the house was being occupied. Their grandmother was only carrying her handbag and the boys were wearing their red scarves as members of the Young Pioneers, a communist youth organization. They made their way to the train station in the dark. When stopped by the guards at the station and asked where she was going, their grandmother proudly announced that she was taking the boys to see Stalin Avenue, a communist showplace in East Berlin. When further pressed, she advised the guard that she wanted the boys to see the progress of the communist party by showing them this avenue that was so hailed in the east. The guard accepted her explanations, recognizing her intention as that of a loyal communist, and so they were allowed to board the train to Berlin.

Once they arrived at the East Berlin station, they had to make their way to the subway station. It was now morning and soon the East German authorities would come to realize that the children had not reported to school, and they would surely begin an immediate investigation and search. A defection to the west would be a dark stain on the communist system and the local authorities who had allowed this to happen.

At the subway station, again armed patrols were stationed throughout and so Grandma and the two boys were quickly intercepted and questioned about their destination. Here again their grandma, while smiling proudly, informed the guard that she was planning to show her two young pioneers Stalin Avenue, so that they could see firsthand the progress communism had made. She seemed confident in what she had said to the guard and he, probably being a good party member himself, could hardly deny them such an opportunity.

The subway system was originally designed to serve the entire city of Berlin, so it made a complete round trip until it reached its original starting point. Berlin was now divided into four sectors, with the Allied forces claiming three sectors. The train still made its complete rounds and stopped at each station, regardless of sector.

Relieved, they now began their final and most dangerous segment of their journey to freedom as they boarded the subway train. Once the train began to move, it would stop at three East Berlin stations before reaching the first two in West Berlin. Following these would be all eastern stations again. East German guards with submachine guns patrolled all the railcars. One of the guards, while passing the two boys, briefly looked at their red scarves and, apparently satisfied, moved to the next car. Now they had to pass one more station before entering the western sector. What would they do if the guard happened to be near them? The train would only stop briefly and if that moment was missed there would only be one final chance. They could not appear too anxious either, as this would surely alert the patrolling guard.

They had just left the last communist-controlled station and the next stop would be the west and hopefully freedom. A guard approached them with both hands resting on the weapon hanging from his shoulders. He continued to walk past them, heading for the next car. The brakes of the subway train began to squeal as the train started to slow down while approaching the next station and freedom. Grandma had talked with the boys to advise them that, once she gave them the signal, they should get off the train without hesitating. The well-lit station now came into sight and several West German policemen were patrolling the platform. Further back off the platform were two American soldiers casually observing the incoming train.

The railcars had now come to a halt and would only stop for seconds before moving on. Grandma had been looking around to be sure that it was safe for them to reach the door of their car. The guard was near the end of the compartment but facing the door to the next car, so he had his back to the three passengers.

"Now!" was Grandma's quiet but firm command as all three headed for the door and, opening it, jumped out onto the platform. The guard now turned around, raising his weapon and realizing that he was too late to stop them. The West German officers immediately took the three escapees into their protection to avoid them being pulled back onto the train. The patrolling American soldiers also came rushing over to assure that the Eastern guard was not allowed to interfere or to force them back onto the train at gunpoint.

"*Got sei Dank! Wir haben es geschaft. Wir sind frei!*" ("Thank God! We have done it. We are free!") was all Grandma could say as she began pulling off the boys' red communist Young Pioneer scarves. Her haste in doing so seemed to demonstrate an urgency to rid herself of anything associated with the system they had just escaped.

Taking the boy's hands, she led them to a nearby bench. While seating herself, she opened her purse, their only piece of luggage. Extracting a handkerchief, she began to wipe the free-flowing tears of relief and joy from her face. The policemen and the American soldiers stood silently just a few feet away, realizing all too well what life-threatening experience this brave woman had just gone through. Their presence also served to convey that no harm would come to this small party now under their care.

West German authorities, with the support of the western Allies, were constantly patrolling the free sector of Berlin and were prepared to assist anyone escaping from the other side. From here the new arrivals were taken to a local processing center for their first meal in the free west. Their names were added to those who had previously escaped from the eastern sector and each was given a gift package containing the necessities for their onward journey to rejoin their family. Following their reception, Grandma and the boys were flown out of Berlin to Hannover in West Germany by means of the air bridge operated by American forces. Here they were reunited with the rest of the anxiously awaiting family.

Karl was closest to my age. He was the oldest of the children and had been one of the last to come over with his grandmother and younger brother. We soon became the closest of friends and have remained so. Our families too were to remain in a close friendship with each other, and so the details of their life-threatening escape often became the topic of discussion during the frequent visits between us. Since our family had been drawn into their confidence since the earliest escape plans had been discussed, we felt a certain partnership with them. Hearing about this dangerous escape was something we never seemed to get tired of.

Although the war had been over for several years, we all experienced its outcome in different ways. It reaffirmed how fortunate we had been to be occupied by American troops and the freedom we enjoyed as a result. For those unfortunate people who were occupied by the Soviets, they were now experiencing a system of repression, lies, and propaganda. Although the name had changed to communism, the system was not so different from what had caused the war in the first place.

* * *

An Explosive Situation

During the fall of 1953, when I was nearly fourteen, our family came into the possession of a used bicycle. It was quite a novelty for us, so we felt somewhat elated by this new possession. Since it had to be shared by the entire family, we each had to await our turn. With each of my turns, I usually tried to make maximum use of the opportunity to ride it. On one of those occasions, my friend Reinhard and I decided to ride to a town about a three-mile distance away. We had just passed through a neighboring village and were now again on the open road to the town of our destination. The road was lined by fruit trees, and just beyond a shallow drainage ditch were freshly plowed fields and pastures stretching all the way to the edge of the distant forest. It was an overcast day and we were in no particular hurry.

Suddenly Reinhard noticed something by the road and quickly applied his brakes. While still moving, he began to turn around. "What is it?" I asked him, following his sudden move. He had now stopped by the side of the road, and as I pulled up beside him, he pointed to an object lying at the edge of the field on the other side of the shallow ditch. "What do you think it is?" I asked, looking at the metal object. Reinhard leaned his bike against the nearest fruit tree and curiously approached the mysterious object. Within seconds I had joined him, and while staring at the object we quickly recognized it as an unexploded cannon shell. It was approximately twenty-five centimeters in length and maybe ten centimeters in diameter, and it came to a point at one end. It must have landed in the soft ground sometime during the war some eight to ten years ago. The farmer must have just recently brought it to the surface when he plowed this field.

It was not unusual to still find ammunition and an occasional unexploded bomb often buried below rubble. In fact, workers had recently discovered an unexploded bomb while digging below the railroad tracks inside a busy train station in a nearby city. Trains had been running over those very tracks since the end of the war. It was assumed that, perhaps following an air raid during the war, quick repairs had been made to keep the station operating. But no one realized the presence of this large, unexploded object embedded in the ground. Upon hearing this news, many began to wonder why the vibration of the heavy trains rolling over it daily did not cause it to explode. Having heard about these frequent discoveries, we looked at each other in amazement and with a certain excitement. "What shall we do?" was the question on both our minds.

"Let's bring it to the police!" was Reinhard's suggestion.

"Maybe we will become heroes for doing so," was my input. Looking again at the object with a new excitement, we realized that we needed a box to better transport this valuable but explosive find.

To enable us to quickly find the location again, we rolled our find into the ditch between the field and the road so it would not be detected by someone else. We then marked the spot with a large rock, just to assure that we could easily find it again. Satisfied with our action, we returned home in search of a suitable carton.

From the small grocery store across the street from us, we were able to obtain a carton that seemed suitable for our project. Our concern now was that the carton might be too small and we would have to come back once again if it turned out to be so. With the help of a string, we quickly secured the carton on the back of Reinhard's bike. We both agreed to deliver our find to the police and were convinced that this would surely be a newsworthy event. Doing so should give us special recognition by the community, we thought. Feeling excited about what we were about to do, we began our ride back to our marked location.

It was a little past four thirty as we arrived back at our important find. The sky had been overcast nearly most of the day but at least it didn't rain. There it was, just as we had left it. We both stopped and quietly looked at it briefly, as if we were reconsidering our previous decision. Reinhard broke the silence. "Will it fit into the box?" he asked, and both of us turned to the cardboard box on the back of his bike.

"How heavy is this thing anyhow?" I asked as Reinhard stepped closer to pick it up.

"It's not too bad!" he replied as he turned to hand it to me. Holding it in my hands, I examined it from its pointed tip to the flat part at the other end. "I wonder why it didn't explode originally," I thought aloud, and while doing so I came to recognize a sense of nervousness in myself.

By now Reinhard had moved his bike closer. "I wonder how much damage this thing could do?" I said, looking at my friend as if he would have an answer.

"It will probably leave a small crater if it explodes," was his reply as he took the shell from my hands.

"Hold my bike steady, I want to see how it fits into the box," he said curiously as he lowered our find into the open box. "The box is actually too big. This thing will roll around inside," was Reinard's somewhat disappointed reaction. "Oh well, it will have to do. We'll just have to take it easy," he stammered as he took the handlebars while staring back at the box.

"I will be right behind you to keep an eye on things," I assured him as I prepared to follow him.

As Reinhard began to mount his bike, I could see the walls of the open carton being pushed out by the rolling content inside and wondered whether the box had been strapped down securely enough. "Be careful not to sway too much. Otherwise this thing can fall out," I shouted after him, looking briefly at the pavement as I started to follow him, keeping a distance of just a few yards. "It's not too bad now," I assured him as we reached a normal pace. While watching the box, I couldn't help wondering if the shell would really explode if it should drop onto a hard surface like the road. After all, it had not exploded when it hit the softer field.

We rode about two miles before we reached the edge of town, and not too much was said. It was previously decided that we would deliver our important cargo directly to the police. The road entering the town from the north side now became the Hauptstrasse. "Boy, if they knew what we have here," I could hear Reinhard exclaim without turning around. He was referring to the people on the sidewalks.

"Well, we are just about there," I said with some excitement as the town hall came into view. As we turned into the small parking lot, Reinhard carefully brought his bike to a stop, dismounted, and gently leaned our find against the wall as I followed behind him.

We were now standing in front of the town hall and deciding our next action. The small police station was located in the basement. As we unfastened the carton, we decided to finish this properly, and so we both took hold of the box to avoid our object from breaking through at the bottom. From here we carried it up the few steps to the entrance of the three-story building. Once inside, we found a short stairway leading to the lower ground level. As neither of us knew the location of the police department, we had to cover several hallways before we finally reached the door that indicated *Polizei* (Police).

This was going to be our great entrance, and surely we would soon be recognized for our heroic efforts. We gently placed the open carton on the floor and nervously, but not too loudly, knocked on the door. Our hearts began to race as we waited for an answer but none came. Reinhard knocked again, a little louder this time. Again, no answer. We repeated this once more but again without any reply from inside. "There is nobody here," I said, somewhat disappointed and looking at Reinhard.

"What do we do now?" he responded, looking at me puzzled.

"We need to come back later," was all I could say as we began to pick up our box. "We could try to find one of the two policemen somewhere in town," I suggested as we reached our bikes outside.

"I have to be home for supper or I'm in trouble," Reinhard exclaimed, looking concerned. I knew that his step-parents were very strict in these matters and so I did not argue with him. As we tightened the carton and its dangerous content back on his bike, we discussed what to do with it, as his parents could definitely not be told. "I will meet you back here after supper and we will see if we can find someone," Reinhard said as he pushed his bike back onto the main road.

"Where are you going to hide this thing?" I called after him and waited for a reply.

"I'll see," he responded as he rode off.

"Be careful," was all I could shout after him. He just raised his hand without turning around, acknowledging my last remark.

It was about an hour later when we met again and I noticed that the carton was no longer tied to the luggage rack of his bike. "Where is the shell?" I asked, looking at Reinhard expectantly.

"I put it in the doghouse with our shepherd. Nobody will be looking in there," he replied, looking somewhat proud of himself.

"Have you told anyone about our find?" I asked, knowing that he would not have mentioned it to his parents.

"No, not yet," was his reply. "Have you?"

"No," I assured him as we began to approach the police bureau once again. Since we had two police officers assigned to our town now, we wondered about which of the two officers would be on duty.

This time we quickly found the door to the police department. After knocking again several times, we disappointedly realized that it was still unattended. Our previous enthusiasm became somewhat dampened as we decided to look around town in hope of finding one or both of the officers. The whole thing had not turned out at all as we had expected. After an additional forty minutes of searching, we finally came upon one of the officers sitting at the bar in one of the oldest restaurant-and-bars in town.

As we excitedly told him of our find, he promptly advised us not to bring the item into town and to leave it where we had found it. At this point we admitted that we had already carried it, not only through town but right up to his office door. From his reaction we immediately realized that we would not be receiving the expected praise. While getting to his feet, he muttered, "Oh my God. Where is it now?" From his stern expression, we realized that this was of a serious concern.

First looking at me with a nervous expression, Reinhard advised the officer of the doghouse location in his backyard. His face had turned to the officer and then quickly toward the ground, as if in preparation for some kind of physical response. Then while looking at both of us with a stern face, the officer instructed us to stay away from the explosive object. While heading for the door, he advised us that he would make the necessary arrangements with the nearest bomb squad for any further handling.

From this serious reaction, we realized that our expected praise was not likely to happen. In fact it now appeared that we could be in trouble with the law and, more importantly, with our parents as a consequence. Since the shell had to be retrieved from Reinhard's doghouse in his backyard, our parents would be advised almost immediately, and so we both stalled going home until nightfall. By then most of the town had already heard the news, as the arrival of the nearby city bomb squad did not go unnoticed.

When I finally dared to go home that evening, I became aware that the police had talked to our parents. Fortunately they had left the matter of advising us of the seriousness of our reckless action to our parents. To our surprise, neither of us received the expected punishment, as our parents were thankful that we had survived the ordeal unharmed.

It was not until several days later that an article appeared in the county newspaper about two youths finding an unexploded artillery shell. It also gave the location where the shell had been found. It further stated that the item had been detonated in a local stone quarry under the supervision of a special bomb squad. As Reinhard and I read the short article, we felt disappointed that after all our efforts not even our names had been mentioned in connection with this serious event.

Other than being able to tell our friends, we learned that there was nothing glorious for us to boast about and the matter was soon forgotten by the community. Reinhard and I would often talk about this event in our life. We had learned through this childhood foolishness about the danger to which we had exposed ourselves and others. How easily and quickly we could have lost our young lives, and perhaps those of others with us, because of this dangerous remnant of the war.

* * *

Epilogue

Writing about these early years of my childhood has allowed me to re-experience them, even if only in my memory. There are those that I have tried to share, while others remain private and only for myself. Although they were difficult years, they remain the most cherished for me. It is surprising how clearly and vividly my memories of even the earliest years have remained with me. The times of fear and the struggle for survival created tight family bonds. It was this family closeness that provided us with the feeling of security during those very troubled times.

While trying to recreate these events from my childhood, I had to remind myself not to allow the feelings of my youth to be influenced by the adult in me. Through our imagination, we, as children, can often create our own world and in so doing are able to temporarily disassociate ourselves from the troubled world around us. This is what set us apart from the adults. During the many frightening times, we relied on Mom for security and protection.

I was glad for her that she had Aunt Mary so close by, who would come across the hall many times during the course of a day. I saw that sharing and discussing their daily problems served them both, and it felt good to see that they could even share an occasional laugh together.

Whatever Mom had to do, it always seemed to be in double time, with seldom a rest until nighttime. I can still picture her trying to push the fallen dark hair strands from her face while scrubbing the family clothing on her old washboard. Even to this day she continues to clean her plate of food at every meal, no matter what. Mom still recalls those difficult years, and for her food is still something sacred not to be wasted. Dad passed away some twenty-five years ago, and Gunter too passed on about three years ago. Mom has continued to live alone in her small home in the town of my birth. She is now ninety-three and still mentally alert. Although my brother Wolfgang and sister Marlene have their own lives, Mom continues to be the matriarch of the family. Her tiny living room often becomes the gathering place for her children, grandchildren, and great-grandchildren. We feel blessed to still have her with us and will never forget what she has done for us under the most difficult of times and circumstances.

Being a father of three grown children myself, I can now much better understand the enormous sacrifices she and other mothers had to make to bring us through those difficult years. In spite of the shortages, she would always find a space and a meal for any relative in need. These were important values for us children to observe and inherit.

The highest military honor bestowed on a German soldier then was the Iron Cross. Yet to the best of my knowledge no such honor was ever bestowed on any mother for doing the best she could on the home front and under the most difficult of circumstances. It was simply expected from the women back home, and so they carried out this important duty of preserving the family with heroism. This applied then and continues to this day.

At the age of twenty, I made my dream of coming to America a reality. Since then I have lived more than two thirds of my life in the United States. It was a decision I have never regretted. Adjusting to a new lifestyle and a different language was at times difficult and yet fascinating. Only four years after arriving here, I found myself drafted and serving in the same army that had liberated us from our own war. It seemed ironic that suddenly I was part of a force that only years earlier had been our enemy and that I had come to admire during our time of occupation.

While serving as a soldier, my thoughts often drifted back to the time of our occupation by American troops. How we used to admire their casual style and their kindness and generosity, especially toward us children, who were always asking for chocolate or gum.

I still find myself reacting when first hearing a large propeller-driven aircraft, as I still associate this sound with approaching bombers. Fortunately, however, this reaction only lasts for an instant and is quickly dispelled.

As for my apprehension of the dark, I never did find a reasonable explanation other than perhaps the memory of the nightly air raids we experienced. It improved with age, and so it may have been just a simple childhood fear, but I still wonder.

In spite of the fact that our childhood years were overshadowed by the events of the war and the difficult times that resulted from it, it is nevertheless a time that all of us who grew up together hold dear. Reunions are always an opportunity for us to relive these events, as everybody has something special to share. After quietly listening, Mom will then usually add her often-mentioned questioning statement: "*That we survived all of that.*"

* * *

Breinigsville, PA USA
29 March 2011
258622BV00001B/58/P